Praise for Stephen and Anita's first brilliant book, *Escape the Rooms*

"Poignant, wildly unpredictable and laugh-out-loud funny" *Daily Express*

"A brilliant, clever, kind of genius book" *Graham Norton, Virgin Radio*

"Richly imagined and deeply heartfelt" *Guardian*

"Manages to feel [...] at the same time [...] *Housekeeping*

"A beautiful and exciting adventure that ignites the imagination" *Edith Bowman*

Published in the UK by Scholastic, 2022
Euston House, 24 Eversholt Street, London, NW1 1DB
Scholastic Ireland, 89E Lagan Road, Dublin Industrial Estate,
Glasnevin, Dublin, D11 HP5F

Text © Stephen Mangan, 2022
Illustrations © Anita Mangan, 2022
Cover illustrations by Anita Mangan

ISBN 978 0702 31500 8

A CIP catalogue record for this book is available from the British Library.

Printed by CPI Group (UK) Ltd, Croydon, CR0 4YY
Paper made from wood grown in sustainable forests and other
controlled sources.

1 3 5 7 9 10 8 6 4 2

www.scholastic.co.uk

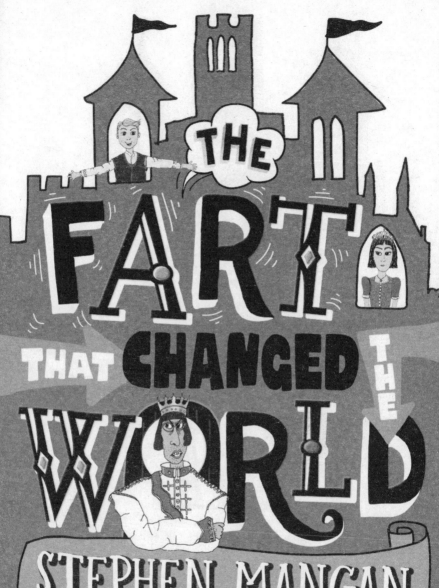

THE FART THAT CHANGED THE WORLD

STEPHEN MANGAN

ILLUSTRATED BY ANITA MANGAN

SCHOLASTIC

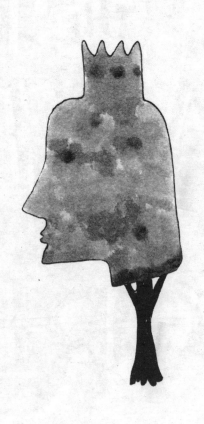

For Louise, who changed my world.

CHAPTER ONE

King Fabian III, the first-born child of King Fabian II and Old Queen Grace, ruler of the kingdom of Gabsland, Grand Master and First Knight of the Ancient Order of the Thistle, Defender of the Faith, Sovereign of the House of Gadsby, Lord Commander of the Army, First Admiral of the Fleet and Custodian of the Holy City, opened his eyes, swung his legs out of bed, stood up, stretched and farted.

He hadn't meant to fart but there it was

1

– tight and high-pitched like a short, sharp note from a bugle.

This was a fart like no other in history.

This was a fart with *consequences*.

This, the inadvertent fart, one summer's morning, from the rear of King Fabian III, was a fart that changed the world.

CHAPTER TWO

Each morning, King Fabian was gently roused from his slumber by his faithful butler, Dimmock.

At precisely 7.23 a.m. Dimmock would leave his shoes outside the royal bedroom and push open the door – well-oiled so that there would be no squeaking hinges.

He would creep across the wooden floor to the large window that looked over the highly-manicured royal garden.

3

Dimmock was not a small man, but he was able to glide across the floor in total silence. He placed each foot as delicately and lightly as a butterfly with a broken toe.

At the window he checked the time again and waited silently until 7.28 a.m.

He was discreet enough not to gawp at the king and queen as they slept, but stood, facing the curtains, his nose lightly pressed against the fabric.

At the right time he began, oh so gently, to pull on the rope hanging to his right and the curtains would begin to open.

So skilled was Dimmock that he could take *exactly* two minutes to open the curtains fully. No more. No less.

As morning light started to filter into the room, brightening it smoothly and slowly, Dimmock would, oh so quietly, begin to make bird noises. His favourite was a wood thrush, not a bird native to the region, but one with a beautiful, melodious sound. At other times he would imitate the fabled song of the nightingale.

Dimmock would start these expert impressions so quietly that they were barely audible and built them in tandem with the curtain opening so that they reached their loudest as the curtain was parted to its fullest.

This was all normally enough to wake the king without startling him, but not always.

If the king still slept, Dimmock would glide over to the royal bed, kneel, and ever so gently blow on the king's royal face. This was a last resort.

Once, maybe twenty years ago, even this had not worked. Dimmock had come up with the idea of tickling the king's exposed right foot with a feather. When the king woke to find Dimmock at the end of the bed stroking the royal foot, he made it clear to Dimmock that this was never to happen again.

Why such an elaborate routine to wake the king each morning? Two reasons.

The king was of a nervous disposition and frightened easily. And, once startled, it could take him a long time to recover. There was the time King Fabian had opened the door to the royal library to find the Bishop of Gabsland unexpectedly standing on the other side of it. King Fabian had screamed for forty minutes and did not stop shaking for twenty-four hours. Another time, the king, startled by someone unexpectedly dropping a plate behind him, ran and hid on the middle shelf of a large fridge. He came out two hours later, shivering and covered in yogurt.

The other reason was that the queen liked to wake up, in her words, "naturally". She could get irritated, if not downright angry, if she was jolted out of her sleep before she was ready.

Dimmock's routine managed to tread the fine line between waking the king and not disturbing the queen.

And today it was important that everything went smoothly. Today the king was hosting the rulers of Gabsland's two neighbouring

countries, Spamon and Hipnia.

The kingdom of Gabsland was a small country compared to the countries which surrounded it. Spamon to the west had a harsh, mountainous landscape and, like its people, was tough and rugged. Hipnia to the east was green and lush and, like its people, appeared soft and gentle.

Appearances, though, can be deceptive.

The Spams and the Hipneys were bitter rivals and had been for as long as anyone could remember. They *hated* each other.

The Hipneys thought the Spams were rude, uncultured and stupid. The Spams thought the Hipneys were weak, self-absorbed and annoying.

In Hipnia, the worst thing you could say to someone was that they were behaving like a Spam, and in Spamon the worst thing you could say to someone was that they were behaving like a Hipney.

One of the most popular jokes in Hipnia was **"How many Spams does it take to change a light bulb? Five hundred – one to hold the bulb and the other four hundred and ninety-nine to turn the house around."**

One of the most popular jokes in Spamon was **"How many Hipneys does it take to change a light bulb? Twenty-one – ten to hold a meeting to decide whether to change**

9

the bulb, one to change it and ten to sing a song about how sad they feel for the old light bulb."

They were always desperate to prove that their country was better than the other.

Many years ago the Spams built a small footbridge over a river made with rope and planks of wood. When the Hipneys heard about this, they built a new, bigger bridge over one of their rivers out of stone. The Spams, not to be outdone, knocked down their rope-and-planks bridge and built one made from steel and painted it bright yellow. So the Hipneys knocked down their stone bridge and built a huge bridge with bronze lamp posts. So the Spams knocked down their steel bridge and built one with gold lamp posts, a row of shops and a swimming pool in the middle. So the

Hipneys replaced their bridge with one that had four different levels, diamond-encrusted benches, formal gardens, a choir singing relaxing music and, halfway across, a foot-massage parlour. The Spams are in the process of designing their new bridge and hope to start building it soon.

What is particularly interesting is that both river crossings are in rural areas and are hardly ever used. The Hipney bridge is only used twice a day by one old woman visiting her grandchildren – once in the morning on the way to their house and then again on her return trip. She's deaf so she can't hear the choir singing, and she hasn't visited the foot-massage parlour once because she doesn't like people touching her feet. But, as their bridge is currently better than the Spam one, the

Hipneys are delighted.

Their rivalry extends to more than bridges. They try to outdo each other in every way. King Fabian, finding himself lacking funds, once borrowed some money from the Spams. As soon as the Hipneys discovered this, they immediately contacted Fabian offering to lend him even more money. Surprised but delighted, he accepted. This led to an offer of a bigger loan from the Spams. And on it went.

The situation now was that the kingdom of Gabsland owed both the Hipneys and the Spams a very considerable amount of money. So much, in fact, that if they both asked for it to be repaid right now, the kingdom of Gabsland wouldn't be able to do so. The sum owed is so vast that if they insisted on it being repaid right now, then the Gabslandians would have to sell the palace, all their national treasures and most of the farmland in their small country. In short, the country would have to be sold, leaving the king and queen and all their subjects with nowhere to live. It didn't bear thinking about.

The Hipneys and the Spams were warily watching each other to see what move the other was going to make. Should they ask for their money back now or should they give the kingdom of Gabsland more time to pay? Neither wanted to appear less generous than the other, but neither wanted to appear more foolish than the other. It could easily go either way.

It was a delicate and tense situation that needed handling in a skilful and sensitive manner. Get it wrong and it would be a disaster.

Luckily, though, Fabian was trusted by the people and renowned as a master negotiator.

Any Gabslandian could tell you the story of the time, five years ago, when the Spams had placed thousands of soldiers on the Gabsland border and everyone was sure they were coming to seize what was owed them. Fabian was the only one, they'll tell you, who remained calm and collected at that tense time. He rode out bravely, oh so bravely, on his own, spoke with the Spams, and told them in no uncertain terms that they were asking for more trouble than they could handle if they even dared to set foot – even one tiny toe – on Gabsland soil. And it worked: they left. Our king, our brave, fearless, clever king did that, the people will tell you.

And when he returned to inform his subjects that the Spams were retreating, what a hero's reception he got! How adored was he by the people! How thrilled and impressed was the queen with her brave husband!

Yes, King Fabian often seemed nervous, inept, indecisive, scared, hopeless, even hapless – but when it really mattered, when the chips were down, he had come through and delivered the goods!

Then, three years ago, disaster had struck again. The Hipneys had attempted to kidnap the king, hoping to force him to repay the loans. Fabian fought off three hundred of their soldiers on his own! It doesn't get braver or more fearless than that! Single-handedly defeated an entire battalion of trained assassins, saving his own life and saving the country. A hero! How admired was he by his people, how thrilled were they to be led by him! How proud was the queen!

But – as you might have guessed – those stories were not *entirely* accurate. In fact, the truth was something else altogether. Only the king and one other person knew what had really happened.

But the king tried not to worry too much about the truth. He had to focus on today – which might be the most important day in the entire history of Gabsland.

To try to get them onside, Fabian had invited the Spam and Hipney rulers to a special Day of Celebration – a celebration of the kingdom of Gabsland and all that it could offer. Hoping to impress his neighbours with the richness and impressiveness of the Gabslandian national traditions and achievements, and in doing so charm the Spams and the Hipneys into not demanding their money back *right* now. They were hoping to show how organized and competent they were so that the Spams and the Hipneys would not worry about being repaid eventually. A careful itinerary had been planned to show the kingdom at its best, to show that it was worth saving. It was a last-ditch, desperate measure and if it didn't work they would have to give everything they had to their neighbours and the kingdom of Gabsland would cease to exist.

So that morning, when Dimmock crept

across the floor of the royal bedchamber, he carried with him a piece of paper. On it was the programme of events for the day. Dimmock had been over it several times, revising and refining the itinerary. He wanted nothing left to chance. Now, he planned to talk the king through, one last time, everything that was planned for the day.

He slipped into the bedroom, waited with his face against the curtain until 7.28 a.m., opened the curtains and made his bird noises. He was halfway through a gentle cock-a-doodle-do when the king opened his eyes, frowned briefly, blinked a couple of times, swung his legs over the edge of the bed, stood up, stretched and farted.

And that was when the trouble began.

CHAPTER THREE

Frank looked over the edge of the boat. The water looked flat and calm and peaceful, but there were sharks down there, he just knew it.

Call it intuition, call it a hunch, but he'd stake everything he owned that beneath the quiet surface swam several fishy killing machines.

Frank had experience with sharks. He knew them. He had a psychic link with them. Sharks and he were forever bonded.

Frank felt a twinge where his right leg used to be. If he didn't know better, he could have sworn he was wriggling the toes on that foot. But there were no toes. There was no leg at all below the knee.

Not for the first time, he wondered where that shark was now. Did the shark think of Frank as often as Frank thought of the shark? The shark had taken Frank's leg, but Frank had taken its eye.

Not "an eye for an eye" – Frank had thought at the time – *but "an eye for a leg".*

his head. *Don't get distracted,* _lf._ That was ancient history. He _us_ on the now.

_wn_ there, maybe five or six metres below the surface, was the sandy floor of the ocean. And somewhere resting on that sandy floor was the key. The key to the wooden treasure chest that Frank had spent two years of his life tracking down.

Was he really going to let a few sharks stop him now? He had come so far, suffered enormous hardships. He wasn't going to throw that away because of a few lousy sharks.

Hell no.

Frank gripped his wooden cudgel tighter in his hand, shuffled to the edge of the boat and, letting out a terrifying blood-curdling scream, dived into the clear turquoise-blue water.

He knew his time was limited. Frank had spent months increasing his ability to stay underwater for long periods. Hours spent holding his breath, increasing the capacity of his lungs, slowing his heartbeat. He reckoned he could stay underwater for maybe six or seven minutes. An extraordinary skill but one that was going to be tested to its absolute limit today.

Looking about, it seemed there was nothing down there with him but a small fish or two. No sharks.

Yet.

He surged deeper: powerful strokes from an expert, natural swimmer. Down he went, feeling the effects of the increased pressure on his lungs, reminding himself to stay relaxed and calm.

23

Scanning the seabed, he made some mental calculations and chose an area to begin his search.

It was dark down here so Frank relied mainly on touch, his left hand busily feeling its way along the ocean floor, quickly rippling across the surface. His right hand gripped the cudgel.

He felt his lungs beginning to tighten. His body was reacting to the lack of oxygen. Frank had to override the compulsion to swim back to the surface to take another breath. He had to defy the panic beginning to surge through him. This was what all those months of training had been leading to.

And then, there it was. The key! Unmistakeably. Small, hard, silver, with a rose-pattern handle. He scooped it up. He had done it! Mission accomplished.

Frank planted his feet firmly on the sandy bottom and prepared to launch himself back up to the light, to air, to freedom.

It was then that he sensed it.

Something was behind him.

He spun round. A dark shadow, moving at high speed, was on him before he could move. Instinctively, he raised his right arm in front of his face to protect himself. A flash of teeth, a burst of bubbles, a malevolent eye—

It took Frank half a second to realize what was happening.

It took him half a second to realize who this was.

And then time stood still for a heartbeat.

The shark and Frank looked at each other. Frank's eyes were wide in surprise. The shark's

25

left eye coldly surveyed him, a scar where the other should have been.

This was Frank's shark.

We meet again, old foe, thought Frank.

"Frank!"

This was the day of reckoning.

"Frank!"

Prepare to suffer, shark-face!

"Frank! FRANK!!!!!"

A hand grabbed Frank by the back of his shirt and pulled him upwards—

"What are you doing with your head in the sink?!"

Cook was so angry she was spitting as she shouted.

"And is that a courgette in your hand? Just wash it and chop it and bring it over to me!"

Frank straightened his apron, gave his wet

head a shake and walked to the chopping board.

"And why are you limping?" yelled Cook. "You pretending to have a wooden leg again?"

Frank said nothing. How to explain where he had just been in his imagination? He began to chop the courgette, his hair dripping pools on to the kitchen floor. The shark would have to wait.

"Honestly!" muttered the cook. **"Most important day in our lives! Cooking for not one, not two, but three rulers and you've got your head elsewhere! Shape up, sunshine! The future of the kingdom of Gabsland is at stake!"**

CHAPTER FOUR

Queen Charlotte was obsessed by death. Most notably her own.

Don't misunderstand – she didn't want to *be* dead. She was very happy to be alive. Life was good – if slightly dull. She loved her daughter, Princess Ella, even if she was a bit moody these days. And her husband, the king, was … fine. But she loved the idea of death: she found a savage beauty in it. She liked to imagine herself languishing in the grip of a picturesque disease on her chaise-longue, preferably in long, flowing robes and pale make-up.

That morning the queen had been woken by something unexpected.

She lay there, eyes closed, fuming. She knew that it was earlier than she would normally wake. She knew that she had not been allowed to wake up naturally. And she knew that it was no ordinary noise which had woken her.

She had grown used to Dimmock's bird noises over the years and they no longer disturbed her. But *this* noise had.

It had been the sound of a fart.

She opened her eyes and sat up.

The king and Dimmock both immediately turned to see if she had been disturbed. They both, she noticed, had stupid little apologetic

smiles on their faces.

"Who..." she began. **"Who made that noise?
Who woke me?"**

Neither of the men said a word.

"Disgusting!" She spat the word with venom.

The king and Dimmock grinned more tightly.

"Well?"

King Fabian began to quiver. He hated the
idea of disappointing the queen. He knew
he disappointed her daily, but he was able to

pretend to himself that she might not notice much of his cowardly behaviour. But now he would have to admit to something that had annoyed, inconvenienced and disgusted her.

Dimmock watched King Fabian and knew immediately what was happening. Fabian was working himself up into a state and that, today of all days, just would not do. Their country needed the king cool, calm and collected. Or at least not openly quivering.

Dimmock did what he knew he had to do: sacrifice himself for his master.

"Apologies, madam," said Dimmock. "I had cauliflower soup for breakfast. It won't happen again."

"Cauliflower soup? For breakfast? Are you losing your grip, Dimmock?"

"Your Royal Highness, please forgive me."

32

The queen scowled. To be woken unnaturally was displeasing; to be woken by a fart, from a servant, no less, was worse. It was *rude*. He needed to be taught a lesson.

"You dare fart in my presence, Dimmock? You disrespect my personage and you disrespect my nose! You wake me from my sleep with that smelly grossness? I think a day in the dungeon for you, Dimmock, a day to reflect on your behaviour. A day to try and learn to control your disgusting gases. A day to achieve some sort of mastery over your bottom."

She rang a bell by the bed to summon the under-butler. Dimmock did not move.

"I am relieving you of your duties, Dimmock, for today. You disappoint me."

King Fabian and Dimmock looked at each

other, both frozen in shock, both horrified, both deeply aware of what this might mean.

It was not Dimmock's place to speak here; he could not contradict the queen. But the king could. This was the king's call and the king, thought Dimmock, *had* to say something.

The two men stared at each other intensely.

To understand what they were thinking in this moment, you need to know what really happened on the two occasions the king bravely "saved the nation". The other person who knew the truth about those events was Dimmock.

*

Let us first examine the incident of the Spam army massing on the Gabslandian border, threatening to seize back what was owed to them. When word reached the palace and King Fabian was informed, he passed out with the shock. Dimmock carried Fabian to the royal bedroom and revived him. When the king came round, he shouted **"We're all going to die"**, ran straight into a wardrobe door and knocked himself out again.

Dimmock placed the king gently on the bed and decided to take matters into his own hands.

Dressing in the king's clothes, with his face wrapped in a scarf, Dimmock went to the stables, got on the king's horse and rode to the border. There he found that there were indeed huge numbers of Spam soldiers, but they were quite clearly on holiday. That part of Spamon is very pretty and it was summer. The soldiers were in swimming trunks, mucking about in the lake, sunbathing, having barbecues.

Dimmock rode up and politely asked the head of the Spam army when they were thinking of leaving. When told they would be gone later that day, Dimmock expressed his thanks and rode home, again in disguise.

Creeping unnoticed back into the palace, Dimmock told the king what had happened.

The king then told the ministers of state that *he* had ridden to the border, had heroically faced off against the Spam ruler and made a series of threats that had scared them all away. He made no mention of Dimmock.

Impressed, the ministers had spread the word and soon a large crowd gathered at the palace, demanding to see their king.

Fabian graciously took his place on the royal balcony and soaked up the adoration of his people, with Dimmock looking on. They never spoke about it again.

From then on, the king placed more and more faith in Dimmock, coming to him for advice on matters of state, seeking his counsel when important decisions had to be made. Dimmock was wise and decisive and canny and his advice was always spot on.

And Fabian was celebrated as a wise and clever ruler.

Fabian, as is the way with these things, soon forgot that he was getting this excellent advice from his butler and started to believe he *was* wise and clever. That he really was the great ruler everyone believed him to be.

*

One day a few years later, the king and Dimmock

were out riding together in the north-east of the country, deep in the forests of Winchmore. They stopped at a river to let their horses drink.

Fabian couldn't read maps but always pretended that he could. He'd examine one for a while, then say, **"So which way would *you* go, Dimmock?"** and Dimmock would point in the direction they needed to go and the king would say, **"Yes, you are correct, Dimmock. That is indeed the right way."** And off they'd ride. It fooled neither of them but made Fabian feel a little smarter.

As the horses drank, Fabian had asked for the map to go through the familiar charade. Dimmock noticed the king was looking at the map upside down, but he said nothing.

Suddenly, a wasp buzzed over to Fabian and slammed into his left ear. Fabian, it will not surprise you to learn, was not a fan of wasps. **"What was that?"** he shrieked and, still fully clothed and clinging on to the map, ran straight into the river.

Fabian, it also may not surprise you to learn, couldn't swim, and the moment he hit the water his panic increased. He began thrashing about in the cool water, which only came up to his waist, shouting, **"I'm drowning! Help!! Dimmock!"**

Dimmock waded in and dragged the king to the bank. Fabian, still in a terrible state, ran off and straight into a low-hanging tree branch, which caught him right in the face.

"Someone hit me, Dimmock!" he cried, running off in another direction, where he was hit square in the face by another tree branch.

By the time Dimmock caught up with him, the king had been hit hard in the face by six branches. His face was black and blue.

Dimmock sat the king down and wrapped him in a blanket while he considered what to do. They had no map (Fabian had dropped it in the river), and with darkness falling they were in great danger. The wolves would soon be out on the prowl and Dimmock had heard that bears hid deep within these forests.

Fabian's bottom lip began to tremble.

"Don't worry, sire," Dimmock said calmly. "You did a brilliant job fighting off that villainous wasp. Do you think you could stand now?"

Then, using the stars to navigate, Dimmock

led them safely home.

Fabian, his face and clothes a mess, was silent all the way home apart from the occasional sniffle. He felt desperately embarrassed. He now had a reputation as a brave and wise king to uphold and he knew he hadn't been brave or wise that day.

As they reached the palace grounds, he told Dimmock to wait in the wood while he rode in alone. Once home, he told everyone that he had been attacked by three hundred Hipneys and he had fought them all off single-handedly. There was no mention of Dimmock, who slipped back into the palace later by the back door.

*

Now, the king stared at his loyal butler in a

state of complete panic. Whatever lies the king had told in the past, he relied totally on Dimmock. And today, the Day of Celebration, the day of the fart, he needed him more than ever. The future of the country was at stake. Fabian couldn't get through this day without Dimmock.

But he couldn't admit that to the queen. If he did, it would mean admitting that Fabian wasn't the wise, clever ruler that he had been pretending to be. It would mean having to admit to his wife that the one thing, the only thing, she admired him for – his strong, calm leadership of the nation – was a lie.

To make matters worse, Fabian was always telling the queen, in private, that Dimmock was useless, that he (Fabian) did all the thinking for the two of them, and that he'd be better off with a lump of coal as a butler. The queen often suggested firing Dimmock, but Fabian would always come up with an excuse – **"I feel sorry for him, poor chap"** – to keep him on.

So when the queen ordered Dimmock into the dungeon for the day … and today of all days … well … that was a big problem for Fabian. What should he do?

The queen looked at Fabian.

Dimmock looked at Fabian.

Fabian gulped.

CHAPTER FIVE

Frank held the giant's eyeball in his hand. It was heavy. He knew the giant would be hot on his tail—

"**You finished peeling those onions?**" yelled Cook.

"**Nearly!**" replied Frank, snapping back to the task at hand.

"**As my old uncle used to say, 'An onion in the hand is worth two birds in the bush,'**" said Cook.

They both jumped when a bell over the

door rang for the under-butler. They had never heard this bell ring before. Dimmock was so competent and reliable that there was never anything for Roger, the under-butler (or the **"under-used butler"** as he was known) to do. Roger had lots of free time in which to indulge his passion – collecting twigs.

"What the...?" said Cook.

"Do you think they rang it by mistake?" asked Frank.

"Go and find Roger. Hurry!" said Cook.

Frank dropped the giant's eyeball and whipped off his apron. He sprinted out the kitchen door, across the courtyard and into the rear garden. He knew where Roger would be and, sure enough, Frank found him standing under the large oak tree looking longingly up at the branches.

"They rang the under-butler's bell," Frank gasped.

Roger's eyes widened and a grin flashed across his face. He had been waiting for this moment for years. He was the understudy who had never had the opportunity to appear on stage. He had always been the bridesmaid, never the bride.

He had watched Dimmock go about his duties with a critical eye. Oh, how differently he, Roger, would act as butler!

Dimmock had no panache! No presence! No charisma! The job needed someone with flair, with pizzazz.

And Roger, Roger knew, was the man to provide it.

"You're on," Frank told him. **"They want you. Something must have happened to Dimmock."**

Roger's nostrils flared, he drew himself to his full height and, throwing his long hair back, he marched towards his destiny. This was it, this was his moment. Into the palace, up the stairs, along the corridor, up some more stairs to the royal bedroom. He threw open the door dramatically, smashing an antique vase in the process, then assumed a wide power stance, hands on hips, nose in the air, and in a booming theatrical voice bellowed:

"YOU RANG, YOUR MAJESTIES? MY NAME IS ROGER. I LIVE TO SERVE AND I SERVE TO LIVE!!!"

The queen, Fabian and Dimmock looked at him.

"Oh, no, no, no!" snapped the queen. "You're awful. And you broke my priceless vase. You can get in the dungeon too."

And with a wave of her hand she dismissed them both. Before the king could gather his thoughts, Dimmock and Roger left the room, walked down to the dungeon and handed themselves over to the dungeon master, who locked them in a cell together.

CHAPTER SIX

Supreme Leader Spudbug narrowed her eyes as her horse trotted through the kingdom of Gabsland's palace gates. She and the rest of the Spam delegation had ridden through the night to get to King Fabian's in time for the breakfast that was to mark the start of the Day of Celebration.

She and her retinue were desperately hungry and weary, but she, and they, refused to show it. Spams prided themselves on their toughness and the harder the conditions, the more they relished it. It was why Spudbug liked to be wakened every morning with a bucket of cold water flung in her face. Anything else just felt too … easy.

Spudbug didn't like things to be easy. She liked drinking rainwater from puddles instead of from a tap, sleeping on the hard ground instead of in a warm bed and brushing her teeth with a twig even though she had a perfectly good toothbrush.

Spudbug had a shaved head and dressed in army fatigues. She wanted to look tough and she had succeeded in her goal.

Her second in command was called Major Junction, an example of Supreme Leader Spudbug's rather basic sense of humour.

Major Junction – whose first name was Tony – was a middle-aged career army man. Neat, respectable, fussy, old school. He was not a big man but he rode a horse that was way too small for him; in fact, it was the smallest horse in the country: a tiny pony. His legs reached the ground when he sat on it. Major Junction had a fear of heights but admitting that to Supreme Leader Spudbug would have been a serious mistake. A fear of heights would have been seen as a weakness and he would never have advanced to the rank of Major.

Rather than sit on a large horse and feel dizzy, he claimed that riding a tiny horse made things more challenging and difficult (which in some ways was true). That went down well with Spudbug.

"I trust we will be arriving ahead of the Hipneys?" Spudbug said to him now. "I want us to be first at that breakfast table."

"All arranged, Supreme Leader."

"We need to be first at all times today. Maintain a psychological edge; let them know we are top dogs."

"Yes, your Supreme Leadership."

"We must crush or be crushed."

Major Junction sighed. He had heard

this many times. **"Of course, your Supreme Leadership."**

Spudbug took a deep lungful of fresh air. It was going to be a good day. Today they were going to show their enemies what was what. She was going to impress and terrify the Hipneys – who, after all, were rumoured to drink herbal tea, use minty bubble bath and sleep for more than two hours a night. Weaklings.

And the Gabslandians? They didn't matter at all.

*

Up in the bedroom, Fabian was finding it hard to breathe.

He had managed to hold it together while Dimmock and Roger left. He had managed a loving smile at the queen as she furiously got out of bed and stormed to the bathroom. He had even been able to walk nonchalantly over to the window and pretend to look out at the gardens in a casual manner.

But now he was struggling.

He wasn't even sure he could get himself dressed without Dimmock, let alone conduct the role required of him today at the crucial Day of Celebration. Dimmock had been the one who had written the itinerary, made all the plans and was going to ensure the smooth running of the whole affair.

Without Dimmock, this day would be a disaster, and the future of his country and his people would be in ruins—

He stopped. He could hear something – the sound of hooves on gravel. He gripped the window sill and looked out over the gardens.

Oh no.

Spudbug and the other Spams were here.

In smart formation and immaculate army fatigues, they trotted down the long drive.

Fabian let out a gasp and fell to his knees.

CHAPTER SEVEN

Frank, exhausted, lifted the lid of the chest and looked at the dazzling collection of diamonds inside. They were breathtaking. The heat was unbearable, and he had expended a huge amount of energy fighting guards to get to this chamber, but he knew he had to hurry. The Pharaoh's men would be here any moment and this time they would have him trapped.

He reached out for the jewels. Then, out of the darkness, a shape loomed up at him. A mummy! Come to life! Frank screamed, the mummy screamed, and—

"Frank, you frightened the life out of me! Stop screaming! Where are those eggs?"

"Yes, Cook. Coming, Cook," said Frank, his mind returning to the kitchen pantry. He selected ten eggs from the tray in front of him, hoping that none of them contained a genie.

"As my old uncle used to say, 'The early bird gets the egg'," said Cook.

As Frank walked back into the kitchen, an unfamiliar bell rang again!

What was happening today?!

"What's going on now?" asked Cook. "Who is that for?"

Frank looked up at the bell board in astonishment.

"It says it's for the kitchen boy."

| BUTLER | UNDER BUTLER | KITCHEN BOY | BELLY DANCER |

"Can't be."

"That's what it says."

"But you're the kitchen boy," she said. "It can't be for you."

Cook and Frank looked at each other.

"What should I do?"

Cook gathered herself. "You better go to the king's bedchamber."

"Really?!"

"Yes. Take off your apron first."

"Me?"

"It rang for you."

"I've never been into the main house before."

"I should think not. You're the kitchen boy."

"So why do they want me now?"

"How am I supposed to know? Just go!! You mustn't keep them waiting!!"

*

Supreme Leader Spudbug stood in front of the front door of the palace and narrowed her eyes. She loved narrowing her eyes. She did it a lot.

Now, she narrowed them a little bit extra. This was not the treatment she had been expecting, even from the insignificant Gabslandians. They had arrived at the main entrance to the palace and there was no one there to meet them.

This didn't bode well. She'd heard that King Fabian was a great warrior and leader, but she was yet to be convinced.

"We could ring the bell?" Major Junction suggested.

"Then do it before I kick it in," Spudbug said.

Major Junction approached the door. There was a bell and a door knocker. *Why do people do that,* he thought. *Which one am I supposed to use? Is there a door knocker because the bell doesn't work? Or is the door knocker purely decorative?* He couldn't show any indecision – not in front of his strong leader.

Just then, behind them, the Spams heard the unmistakeable sound of the Hipneys approaching. They were singing their national anthem, **"All the Flowers of the Forest and All the Animals of the Earth Are Precious and So Are Rivers".**

"Junction..." growled Spudbug.

And, taking a deep breath, Major Junction

pressed the bell.

Then, for good measure, he banged the door knocker.

*

Up in the royal bedroom, Frank was trying to digest the news.

"You want me ... *me* ... to be the butler?"

The queen didn't hide her impatience.

"Yes, you. Just for the day. The other two are in the dungeon, there's no one else."

"The dungeon? Why?"

"One farted and one ... never mind why ... just go and smarten up. The Spams and the Hipneys will be here any minute."

They heard the doorbell ring and then the door knocker being hammered.

King Fabian rushed to the window and peered out.

"It's Spudbug! She's here! She looks cross! Oh my! And look! There's the Hipneys coming down the drive! They're both here! Together! This is a disaster! Must get ready!"

Fabian, panicked and shaking, ran into the royal dressing-room and slammed the door. Except, he ran into a cupboard by mistake. The door closed on him and he couldn't get out. There was no handle on the inside.

"I'm locked in the cupboard! I can't get out!" he shouted.

Frank and the queen looked at each other. This wasn't quite what Frank had expected from his wise and brave king.

"Here," said the queen. She handed him a crumpled piece of paper. **"That idiot Dimmock**

dropped this. It's the itinerary for the day."

Then she swept off to the bathroom. As Frank listened to the king making increasingly frantic scrabbling noises inside the cupboard, he examined the itinerary.

9.00 — Arrival of rulers. They must not arrive together. Arrange for staff to meet them and escort to separate entrances.

9.30 — Breakfast including many rare Gabslandian delicacies. Dietary requirements must be respected. During the meal there will be exchanging of gifts.

11.00 — Inspection of the troops. A demonstration of our military might. Do not let the king draw his sword, raise his musket or speak.

12.00 — A display by Your Majesty's royal acrobatics troupe, the Gabslandian Gliders.

1.00 — Luncheon

2.30 — Releasing of a thousand peace balloons with King Fabian's face on.

3.00 — An unveiling of a moving new statue, followed by a fireworks display.

"All right," muttered Frank. "That looks doable."

It was time to meet the rulers.

CHAPTER EIGHT

Major Junction, still hammering the front door knocker, nearly fell through the door as Frank opened it.

Junction composed himself as best he could.

"Your, um, Royalness!" said Frank, flustered. "Welcome to my humble kingdom."

Major Junction stared at him.

"Sorry, wait, not *my* humble kingdom. That's not right. Welcome to the king's humble kingdom!"

Major Junction raised an eyebrow.

Frank became increasingly nervous. **"What a beautiful day! How was your journey?"**

Major Junction narrowed his eyes. He'd seen the Supreme Leader do it and thought it looked cool.

Frank squirmed and tried again. **"I like your moustache."**

"Listen, young fellow, we have been riding all night," said Major Junction in a low, menacing voice. **"We need food and water for our horses, showing to our rooms and then some breakfast would be nice. Just some plain bread and water for the Supreme Leader. But first – because you don't seem to know the first thing about welcoming state visitors in Gabsland – you need to go and bow to the Supreme Leader Spudbug and offer a humble welcome."**

"Oh, right!" said Frank. "Thank you."

He walked past Junction and bowed low in front of Supreme Leader Spudbug.

"Welcome... um... "

He couldn't remember her name. Supreme something...

"Welcome... "

Was it Chicken Supreme? Surely not.

Spudbug narrowed her eyes.

They like narrowing their eyes, these people, thought Frank.

"Welcome... um..."

"Supreme Leader Spudbug, how delightful to have you here. You are most welcome."

Frank spun round. It was Princess Ella. She was about the same age as Frank and, despite living in the same palace and helping to prepare all her meals, he had never

spoken to her before. She was so neat and tidy, thought Frank, especially compared to him: her hair carefully cut, a simple but expensive looking necklace round her neck, shoes with delicate little bows. Ella curtsied. Frank followed her example before wondering whether it was correct protocol for kitchen boys to curtsy.

"You must be exhausted," Princess Ella continued. **"Please allow us to feed and water your horses. They will be well taken care of."**

She looked meaningfully at Frank.

"On it," he said gratefully.

"And if you'd like to follow Daisy here, she can take you to your rooms so that you may freshen up before breakfast." She gestured to her maid, Daisy, standing behind her with cheeks flushed red with embarrassment. Daisy looked at Frank as if to say **"What are you doing out here?"** Frank tried to look as if he often spent time at the front door, welcoming the ruler of Spamon to King Fabian's palace. His heart was hammering in his chest. He was not cut out for this.

"We did not expect to be greeted by Your Royal Highness," said Spudbug gruffly.

"But of course. You are important guests," said Ella. **"We want your stay here to be as pleasant as possible."**

Ella looked at Frank who was still curtsying. She nudged him.

"Kindly see to the horses ... er..."

"Frank."

"Frank. Yes."

Ella smiled as the Spams marched past, then whispered in Frank's ear.

"Have you noticed the Hipney delegation coming? Over there. Don't look. I can tell by their awful singing. Let's just get this lot out of the way and we can deal with them after. The important thing is we need to stall them till all the Spams are inside."

"Why?" asked Frank, helplessly.

Ella rolled her eyes. "Because they hate each other and have been bitter rivals for decades. They should never have been allowed to arrive at the same time as the Spams," she said. "We were lucky they didn't start fighting right here. I can't believe Dimmock let that happen. As a matter of fact – where *is* Dimmock?"

"In the dungeon."

"What?! Why?"

"The rumour is he farted."

"Don't be revolting."

They watched as the Hipneys made their way through the topiary garden of the palace, stopping every so often to examine the planting. The garden was famous throughout Gabsland and on the few days a year that it was open to the public, thousands travelled from far and wide to see the famous plant sculptures. Trees, shrubs and bushes had been trained and trimmed into all sorts of fantastical shapes and figures. Frank thought it was magical. Although strictly not allowed to visit the garden, Frank often snuck out at night to wander through

the incredible shapes. There were pyramids, spheres and boxes. There were animals – an elephant, two giraffes and a rhino – as well as faces, figures and, the one Frank loved the most, a sailing ship, all fashioned out of living plants. Frank realized the Hipneys had stopped singing and were looking rather upset.

"**What's wrong with them?**" Frank asked.

The princess sighed.

"**I think they're upset about the plants,**" she said. "**Dimmock warned us this might happen.**"

Frank couldn't understand how the Hipneys could think of the garden as anything but magical.

"**Do these plants want to be used in this way?**" one was saying loudly. "**To conform as sculpture? To be trimmed against their will?**"

"**Yeah!**" shouted one particularly hairy Hipney who, Frank thought, looked as if he could benefit from a trim of his own. "Leave the plants to grow in a natural way! Who are we to impose our human values and beliefs on plants!? Plants don't expect us to grow leaves and branches so why do we expect plants to look like" – he looked at the topiary he was standing next to – "like a pyramid! It's wrong! FREE THE PLANTS!"

"FREE THE PLANTS!" everyone started chanting. "FREE THE PLANTS!"

One of the Hipneys held up her hand. "We are about to enter the royal palace. Can we check in on everyone's feelings before we continue?"

The hairy Hipney thought for a moment. "Maybe I don't want to share my feelings at this time?"

"Don't you?"

"Can I get in touch with

74

my feelings and get back to you?"

"Sure."

The princess leaned over to Frank. "We need to speak to them. Let me do the talking. They sound soft, this lot, but they can be savage. Believe me."

Princess Ella slowly approached the Hipneys, a broad grin on her face.

"Welcome!" she said. "How wonderful to have you all here. Whom should I address?"

A man stepped forward.

"I am No Better Than Anyone Else," he said. "Or Simon, for short."

Frank thought that was a strange way to introduce yourself but Princess Ella seemed to understand what he had said.

"You are most welcome, as are you all," said

Ella. "You must be tired after your journey. Would you like to be shown to your rooms before breakfast is served?"

The Hipneys – there were ten of them – moved into a huddle.

"Right," said Simon. "We're going inside, right? It's why we're here after all."

"Wait!" said another. "Not so fast. I suggest we go on a mountain retreat for a few days to take a breath and properly consider what it is we are being asked here and how we feel about it. After, say, a week of calm reflection, we could consider it."

"I appreciate your thoughts," said another. "But a week is inadequate. Ten days, surely."

"Eight days of reflection and one of bonding, perhaps—"

"Listen," interrupted Simon. "We've come

a long way specifically to attend this event and I'm also really hungry so I suggest, with respect to all the various positions and viewpoints and so on, that we accept their kind offer of breakfast and we can continue to discuss these issues while we eat."

There was silence. The others looked from one to the other, waiting for an indication of which way the group was going to go on this issue. No one wanted to express an opinion that was going to go against the crowd.

After a moment, someone's tummy rumbled and they all began to chuckle.

"There's our answer!" said one.

"Bernadette's stomach has spoken!"

Simon was a large man, the tallest of the group by some margin. He held himself as though trying to deny his height. He was stooped, his neck thrust out and down, his shoulders hunched. He turned to Princess Ella.

"Thank you. We would love some breakfast." He smiled shyly. "It is currently my turn to be leader of the Hipneys. We change leader every three months and no one can be leader twice. We like to give everyone a turn, you see. Whoever is the leader assumes the title of No Better Than Anyone Else. You can call me No Better Than Anyone Else or you can call me Simon."

What a deep voice he has, thought Frank. *Incredibly deep. I can feel my bones vibrating.*

"My second in command is No Better Than Me," Simon said, indicating a painfully shy woman to his left. **"Her real name is Googie."**

Googie just looked at her feet. She fiddled with the hem of her tunic.

They waited for a moment, and then Princess Ella jumped in.

"Please, do come in. You must be exhausted."

Ella led them across the garden to the palace. Frank trotted along beside her.

"They seem nice," he said. **"Nicer than the other lot."**

"Don't be fooled," said Ella. **"They are fine until you do something they disapprove of and then they can be absolutely vicious."**

"Really?" said Frank, looking at Simon lolloping

along with Googie.

"Oh, and something else," said Ella, "I just saved your neck back there."

"I know. Thank you," said Frank.

"And now you owe me," continued Ella. "I might want something from you in future. OK?"

"Of course," said Frank. But there was something in the way Ella said it that sent a shiver down his spine.

"Now go and get properly dressed," she continued. "If Dimmock's really in a cell and we really have to rely on my father ... well, let's just say things could get interesting. You need to look like a butler and start acting like one too." She glanced over her shoulder at the Hipneys. "It's going to be a long day."

CHAPTER NINE

The first item on the itinerary was a breakfast for the king, queen and the highest ranking diplomatic guests.

The dining room was an austere and formal place. Dark oak panels lined the wall; the long dining table, capable of seating forty guests, ran down the middle of the room, with twenty high-backed heavy chairs on either side.

On the walls were mounted the heads of animals that had been hunted and killed by

the king's father, Fabian II. Deer, antelope, wild boar, one tiger, two zebras and a brown bear. All shot by one man over the course of many years.

His son, the current king, Fabian III, had never liked these animals staring down at him as he ate his meals. He felt they were silently saying **"How come you get to live and eat and drink and we have to watch from up here?"** Their beady eyes had bored into the young prince's soul, making him feel desperately uncomfortable.

He never spoke to his father about these animals. His father was an angry, short-tempered, short-lived short man with no time for feelings or emotions. He treated his only son with contempt because the young prince was both sensitive and emotional, and that irritated the older Fabian.

Once his father had died and
the young Fabian became king, he
could easily have had the animal
heads taken down, but he felt unable
to stand up to his father even then. So he tried
to cheer things up by putting party hats on them
and contorting their mouths into grins.

It didn't cheer things up. The animals
looked like they were smiling sarcastically.

Now, the door burst open and Frank slid
into the room. Cook had found an old suit
of Dimmock's for him. It was far too big for
Frank. The trousers had had to be rolled up
at the bottom, as did the sleeves. Frank's
shoulders could have been twice as wide as
they were and they still wouldn't have filled the
space available inside the jacket. Frank had no
black shoes so he had tried to apply black shoe

polish to his white trainers. That had been a
mistake. The polish sat in uneven streaks on
the surface. His shirt was similarly too big. You
could have dropped a small melon into the gap
between the collar and Frank's neck.

Frank took in the room. He had never seen inside before. Just being in here made him feel nervous. Everything was so grand and ornate.

He often asked Dimmock exactly what the king, queen and princess talked about during their meals. Frank imagined that royalty must have the most fascinating conversations; they had seen and done so much in their lives. Did they tell tales of their illustrious ancestors? Did they discuss the difficulties of running the country and how best to solve problems for the good of the people? Perhaps they talked about different rulers around the world that they admired and respected? It must be amazing to listen in on such interesting people.

Dimmock had always been far too discreet to reveal even a fragment of what he had heard over the years.

But now Frank was to be in the room with the royal family! Not just the royal family, but two other leaders and all sorts of important people! He reminded himself that this was a once-in-a-lifetime opportunity and he told himself to relish every moment and remember *everything*.

Frank was also feeling very anxious. What if he messed up? At least Dimmock, being supremely organized, had laid out the place settings the night before, all ready for breakfast. Frank could not believe how many forks, knives, spoons and glasses there were for each person. No wonder there was always so much washing-up to do!

The door opened, making Frank jump. He put his hands behind his back in what he hoped looked like a professional manner, stuck his chin out and threw his shoulders back as

Cook had told him and tried not to blink too much in case the king didn't like blinking.

King Fabian and Queen Charlotte came in. *She looks very pale*, thought Frank.

Fabian walked the queen to one end of the table and then sat down at the other end. Picking up his napkin, he gave it a flick and laid it across his lap.

Frank wondered if he should say something but decided against it. *Only speak if spoken to*, Cook had said.

King Fabian cleared his throat. Frank was rigid with excitement and nerves. If only his parents could see him now. He was about to hear the wisest and bravest man in the kingdom speak.

"That rash on my bottom is still there," King Fabian mumbled.

The queen closed her eyes and gave a faint sigh.

89

"Must have put half a tube of ointment on it every day. Not that it's done any good," said the king after a moment.

Another pause.

"I hope it's not going to linger like that foot fungus I had last year."

The queen said nothing. Fabian looked out of the window and sighed.

"You remember that fungus, dear? My feet smelled like off milk for most of the summer."

King Fabian straightened one of the knives in front of him.

"I was peeling dead skin off my left foot in strips."

The door opened again and Princess Ella stomped in.

"Good morning, sweetie!" said the king.

"Is it?" said Princess Ella.

"Well, yes," said the king. "Breakfast time. Morning."

"WHY DO YOU HAVE TO BE SO LITERAL ABOUT EVERYTHING?" yelled Ella.

Frank's eyebrows shot up in surprise. How could she talk to the king like that? The king! And while he had a rash on his bottom too. The Ella he had met outside had been quick-thinking, resourceful and slightly intimidating – but she hadn't seemed angry.

"Now, now, sweetie!"

"DON'T CALL ME SWEETIE!" shouted Ella, "I'm not made of sugar. My name is Ella."

She folded her arms and clenched her jaw. Her father was the only person who made her behave like this and she had no idea why. Her mother was weird and not really there most of the time so they didn't have much to do with each other. Her father did take an interest in her, though, and he often told her how much he loved her. For some reason he made her irritable and annoyed.

She wished she didn't have to be the grown-up in her family. She just wanted to be the child. She wanted her parents to be the responsible ones. But somewhere along the way it had fallen to her to look out for them rather than the other way around. Her grandfather had been such a strong character – maybe that was the problem. Despite being the king of a country and its ruler, her father was still that little boy who was afraid of his dad.

So Ella had to fill in the gaps and be the adult in the family. Families are strange, she often thought, and every family, she had noticed, is strange in a different way. Still, her family was the only family she had. This was the one she had been born into so she was determined to make the best of it. What else could she do? But sometimes, like this morning, she felt frustrated.

"I had to stop a situation from developing on the driveway this morning. The Spams and the Hipneys arrived at the same time and there was no one there to meet them," she said.

"I sent that boy," protested the king. "The one with the eyebrows."

"Him," said Ella, pointing at Frank. Frank blushed. "OK. I meant there was no one there to meet them who knew what they were doing."

"What did the boy do?" said the king. "Shall I have him thrown into the dungeon?"

Frank began to shake. This was not going the way he had hoped.

Ella put her head in her hands. "Where's Dimmock?" she asked.

"Dungeon," said the king.

"Roger?"

"Dungeon."

"So Frank's the butler? Today of all days?"

"Yes," said the king. "Dungeon?"

"No, because then there won't be anyone to serve us."

"Good point. Dimmock!" the king called.

Frank wondered if he meant him.

"Dimmock, coffee!" shouted the king again.

Frank decided he probably did mean him, so he stepped forward to look for the coffee pot. He had washed it a thousand times so knew it well. He poured the king a cup of coffee.

The door opened and in walked the Bishop

of Gabsland. He had a large round face like an owl, a tiny mouth and large round eyes that always looked full of wonder.

"Morning, Your Majesty," said the bishop to the king. "Good morning, Princess Ella. Good morning, Your Royal Highness."

The queen didn't move. The bishop rolled his eyes.

"Don't catch your death, duckie," he said tartly under his breath. There was clearly no love lost between the queen and the bishop.

"The Spams are ready for breakfast, Your Majesty," he said. "Shall I bring them in?"

"Ah, good morning, Bish," said the king. "Yes, do show them in. But give me a chance to go through the itinerary with Dimmock first."

The bishop looked at Frank.

"You mean him with the eyebrows?"

"Yes."

"**Righto**," said the bishop and left the room.

The king snapped his fingers at Frank and Frank ran over to him.

"**Talk me through it, Dimmock.**"

Frank didn't know if the king had lost his mind and couldn't tell the difference between him and Dimmock or whether he just called all butlers Dimmock. Either way, Frank wasn't going to correct him.

Frank produced the itinerary from his pocket and unfolded it.

"**First, your royal majesty, we have breakfast.**"

"**I know that.**"

"**A spread including many Gabslandian delicacies – onions on toast, cheese and orange sandwiches, banana and garlic soup...**"

"Plenty of garlic!"

"Yes, sire. During breakfast there will be an exchanging of gifts."

"Oooh, I love gifts," said Fabian. "What's next?"

"This will be followed by the inspection of the troops. A demonstration of our military prowess."

"Yes, correct. Our, er military prowess."

"Then a display by Your Majesty's royal acrobatics troupe."

"Splendid."

"Then the release of a thousand peace balloons, and we end with the unveiling of the topiary statue commissioned especially for the occasion – which I'm sure will be extremely moving – and the fireworks display."

The king sat up and gasped. "The statue

will be *moving*, Dimmock?"

"Er ... no, it's a statue."

"But you said ... extremely moving?"

Frank blinked at his paper. "I think it just means ... emotional, sire."

"Aha! Of course! I knew that!" The king laughed loudly.

Ella dropped a spoon which clattered on to the table. Fabian jumped.

"Ella! Stop it! My nerves! Now listen, Dimmock," he said, "the future of the country is at stake today. This is big. This is huge. We all need to be on our best game, yes? We need to stay calm and we need to stay focused."

The door flew open and Supreme Leader Spudbug and Major Junction strode in.

Fabian screamed.

"**Please don't kill me!**" he shouted and disappeared under the table.

Spudbug stopped in her tracks and glared around the room.

The queen still had her eyes shut, Princess Ella closed hers in embarrassment, the bishop followed them in and made a sign of the cross.

Frank felt he should do something.

"**Ha ha ha! Your Majesty, that is a *very* funny story!**" he said. "**'Please don't kill me!' – priceless! What a great anecdote.**"

Frank smiled at Spudbug.

"**And, Your Majesty, Supreme Leader Spudbug is here; perhaps you would like to say hello?**"

The king came out from under the table.

"**Ah, yes, Supreme Leader Spudbug. Welcome. Please sit.**"

Spudbug narrowed her eyes. She did not like King Fabian one bit. He was the very definition of wishy-washy.

Major Junction held out a chair for her and she dropped on to it. Junction took his place next to her.

"Coffee?" asked Frank.

"Black, no sugar," barked Spudbug. "Actually, scrap that. Do you have any dirty dishwater?"

"Dirty dishwater?" asked Frank.

"Yes, it's full of iron. In a glass."

Frank tried not to gag.

"Dirty dishwater. Certainly. Would you like ice with that?" he said.

"No," said Spudbug. "Why would you have ice with that?"

"No reason. And you, sir?" Frank asked Major Junction.

Major Junction was longingly eyeing the banana and garlic soup and other delicacies that had been laid out. Then he shook himself. "I'd like the same please."

"Two dirty dishwaters, coming right up." Frank walked slowly to the door and then ran as fast as he could down to the kitchen.

CHAPTER TEN

In the dungeon, Dimmock sat with his head in his hands. There was no way of telling what the time was, but he reckoned they had only been in the cell for about an hour and he was not sure he could take any more. He had always known that Roger was annoying – but he hadn't realized he was *this* annoying.

"And another thing," continued Roger, **"why do you take such little strides when following the king? Makes you look weak. Own it, man. Show them who's boss."**

"The king is the boss," said Dimmock and immediately wished he hadn't. He wondered whether the Spam and Hipney leaders had arrived. He wondered whether the king was following the itinerary.

"That's your problem, right there!" boomed Roger. **"You have to assert yourself, man! Let**

me show you."

Roger leapt to his feet. He had already shown Dimmock how to hold a tray because he thought Dimmock was doing it wrong. He had demonstrated how to assertively-yet-graciously open doors, how to bow low but not too low, how to pour water from a jug at just the right angle, how to laugh at a joke with exactly twenty-five per cent obsequiousness. Roger clearly felt that everything Dimmock did as royal butler was wrong.

"Watch, Dimmock!" Roger marched up and down the small cell, arms swinging, legs akimbo. **"Work it! Check me out! You need to work it!"**

Dimmock sighed. This was going to be a long day.

*

"And then every morning at 4 a.m., I run fifteen times up and down Spamon's largest mountain, carrying an adult pot-bellied pig on my back."

Supreme Leader Spudbug had drunk two glasses of dirty dishwater and was now telling King Fabian about her new exercise routine.

"Oh, ah – that does sound bracing," murmured the king.

Fabian wasn't good at conversation at the best of times and exercise was something he knew nothing about: he never did any himself. He looked beseechingly around the table but got no help from the rest of his family. The queen had not opened her eyes once, the princess was sitting sulkily with her arms folded, and the bishop was reading the Bible.

Frantically, Fabian tried to recall everything he knew about the Spams. As a child he often had to travel with his father to Spamon to take part in diplomatic visits, which mainly involved hunting and fishing parties, neither of which he enjoyed.

"We are on these trips to develop a friendship with the Spams. We have to fit in," his father would tell him. **"The more they respect us, the greater the chance of a quiet life."**

On these trips Fabian would watch the way the Spams behaved. The adults constantly made jokes by pointing out each other's flaws and laughing about them. Being rude and horrible to people seemed to be what the Spams found funny.

At that time, the Supreme Leader of

Spamon was Gunter, a brutally strong man with the thickest neck and the biggest hands Fabian had ever seen. Fabian desperately wanted to make Gunter laugh, and therefore impress his father.

One day, in the middle of a boring hunting trip, Fabian had pointed at Gunter.

"What did your left eye say to your right eye?" he asked.

"I don't know," said Gunter suspiciously.

"Between us, something smells," said Fabian, giggling. His laughter faded as Gunter took a menacing step forward. **"Because ... in between your eyes ... is your nose,"** Fabian said weakly. **"And it smells."**

It had taken four men to get Gunter off Fabian. Every time Fabian tried to explain the joke, Gunter would pounce again. In the end,

Fabian gave up and never tried to make a Spam laugh again.

Not that his trips to Hipnia with his father had been much better. These were very different to his Spamon experiences but no less awkward.

The first trip involved camping in the woods. For three days their Hipney hosts drank nothing but mushroom soup and had long conversations with the trees. Fabian and his father had been bored out of their minds but had to keep smiling so as not to appear rude.

Fabian was roused from these reminiscences by the return of the new Dimmock – or whatever his name was.

"Excuse me, sire," murmured Frank, carefully depositing fresh glasses of dirty dishwater in front of Spudbug and Major Junction. **"The Hipneys are here for breakfast."**

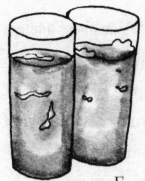

Spudbug snorted. **"Better late than never, I suppose."**

Simon and Googie walked in. Quickly, Frank whispered their names into Fabian's ear.

Fabian sat upright. **"Ah! No Better Than Anyone Else and No Better Than Me! How delightful to see you again! Please take a seat! Welcome!"** he said to the two Hipneys. **"You know my wife, Queen Charlotte."** He nudged his wife gently and she slowly opened one eye, took in the visitors, and waved a languid hand. **"You also know Princess Ella, my sweet daughter."** Ella nodded and smiled. **"And the Bishop of Gabsland. And Supreme Leader Spudbug and Major Junction."** Fabian waved a hand at the vast spread of delicacies. "Please, do let my butler know what you would like to eat – you must be hungry."

"Thank you. Good morning. As you know we don't eat dairy," said Simon.

Spudbug rolled her eyes. "Here we go," she muttered.

"That won't be a problem."

"Or gluten."

"We can handle that."

"Or sugar."

"Dairy, gluten and sugar. Got it."

"Or meat."

"OK. Dairy, gluten, sugar and meat."

"Or fish and yeast."

"Right. No salmon and cream cheese sandwiches then! Ha!"

"Or salt."

"Salt."

"Starch."

"Yep."

"Or eggs, fruit, any food that begins with the letter 'W', coffee, tea, yellow food or nuts."

"I see." Fabian took a deep breath. "What *do* you eat?"

Ella jumped in. "How about some lentils? I know they're a firm favourite."

Simon and Googie conferred for a moment, then nodded. "That would be delightful."

"Cook will whip some up in a moment," said Frank, shooting Ella a grateful look. He sped out of the room.

There was an uneasy silence after Frank had left. Spudbug moodily stirred her dishwater and Simon examined his fingernails.

Ella nudged her father. "What does it say

to do next on the itinerary?" she whispered.

Fabian consulted the piece of paper. "Ah! A pleasure to have you both here. I hope this Day of Celebration will be productive and, er, jolly good fun."

Spudbug snorted into her drink. Simon rearranged his knife and fork.

Fabian scanned his paper again. "Gifts! Of course. Shall we begin with the Exchange of Presents?"

"Of course. No Better Than Me," said Simon to Googie, "do you have the present for our gracious host?"

"With respect, King Fabian," began Googie, "may I first say a few words?"

"Here we go," sighed Spudbug. "Nothing is ever simple with you lot, is it?"

"Simple?" smirked Simon. "Basic? You'd

know all about that."

The two leaders glared at each other.

"I was going to say," interrupted Googie, "that before we give you our gifts, I feel obliged to tell you that we find a system in which complete power is vested in a solitary individual, an autocratic monarchy, antithetical to good governance."

"What?" said Fabian, totally confused.

"Swallowed a dictionary?" said Spudbug.

Simon sighed. "What Googie is saying, is that we don't like kings and queens being rulers," he said.

"Well," said Fabian. "That feels a bit, shall we say, rude, to come here and say something like that at my own breakfast table. After all, I am a king, you know?"

"Googie was going to add that even though

we don't like the idea of kings and queens ruling just because they happen to be born into it," said Simon, "you are always a gracious host. So thanks for that." He cleared his throat. "Perhaps there is a conversation to be had about our two countries working together..."

"Hey! None of that!" shouted Spudbug. "I thought we had agreed to keep things civil. Not to get competitive? You did agree that too, didn't you?"

"Yes," said Simon. "Actually I believe we agreed to that before you did."

"Are you boasting that you won the race to be first to promise not to be competitive?"

"I'm just stating a fact," said Simon.

"And smirking while you do it!" shouted Spudbug.

"Oh, please, don't start an argument

already, for goodness' sake!" implored Fabian.

"Well ... whatever," said Simon. "We brought you two cakes."

He nudged Googie, who walked round to Fabian and placed two cupcakes in front of him.

"My mum made them," said Simon.

Spudbug gave a mirthless laugh. "Is it a dairy-free, wheat-free, sugar-free, egg-free and gluten-free cake then? Count me out."

"Ah. Well, how kind of her," said Fabian, looking nonplussed. Unsure what else to do, he picked one up and shoved the whole thing into his mouth.

Everyone looked at him in disgust.

"Sthddggy," he tried to say, lumps of cake falling out of his mouth on to the table. "Shchhffyd."

Spudbug and Simon looked at each other, bonded for a brief moment by the revolting spectacle.

"That's disgusting," mouthed Simon.

"For once, I have to agree," replied Spudbug.

"Er," said Ella, wondering whether she could salvage the situation. "Can I get you a napkin, Dad?"

Fabian raised a finger as if to say "wait a minute". Minutes passed as he chewed through the block of cake.

After a good ten minutes, he forced it down.

"What I was trying to say was 'stodgy'. Nice cake, bit stodgy."

He reached for the second cake.

"Don't do it, Fabian," said Spudbug. "Or we'll still be sat having this breakfast at lunchtime."

"Whatever you say," said Fabian, pushing the cake away with relief. "Right, thank you. That was a truly unique gift."

"My turn," said Spudbug, sounding bored. She threw a wrapped box on the table. "A necklace. I hear it's worth something. The major is the one who sorts the gifts." Major Junction nodded impassively.

"Oh, thanks," said Fabian, fumbling with the tape.

"Why don't you open it later," said Googie, gently moving the box aside. "That looks quite difficult to unwrap."

"Nice country you've got here, Fabian," said Spudbug. "I don't suppose you'd consider a union?"

"A – a union?" said the king uneasily.

"A joining together of two nations," said Spudbug, showing her teeth. "**Your nation and my nation. Only your nation wouldn't be a nation any more – it would be part of my nation. We could come to a nice arrangement about the money you owe us.**"

"What?" protested the king.

"**Hang on a minute,**" spluttered Simon. "What about *our* money?"

"**Oh, that's typical of you,**" said Spudbug. "**Copying everything we do.**"

"**Of course we don't,**" snapped Simon. "**You copy us!**"

Spudbug snorted. "**Do not.**"

"Do too."

"Do not."

"Do too."

"Right," Fabian interjected. He wished Dimmock was here. Not the new Dimmock, but the original Dimmock who was stuck in the dungeon instead of helping him with international negotiations.

Queen Charlotte suggested that now might be a good time for the rulers of Spamon and Hipnia to exchange gifts.

Simon stood up and faced Spudbug.

"We, the People of Hipnia, would like to offer you, The People of Spamon, the gift of openness, contact, affection, emotional warmth, joy and trust," he said.

"What?" snorted Spudbug. "What does that mean?"

"A hug," replied Simon. "We want to hug you."

"Are you trying to be funny?" said Spudbug. "A hug??"

"That's right. An extended holding. To show our sincerity, our desire to welcome and to connect with each other."

"No thanks," said Spudbug.

"But..."

"No hugging," said Spudbug curtly. "Right, our present–"

"We want to hug you."

"Well, I want to be able to fly, but we don't always get

what we want. So, our present is a great delicacy in Spamon and much sought after." She jerked a head towards Major Junction, who handed her a jar. "Fermented dishwater. Matured for nine months. You'll love it."

Ella dropped her head into her hands.

"I think it's all going pretty well, don't you?" whispered Fabian.

CHAPTER ELEVEN

Frank arrived with a dish of lentils for Simon and Googie and fried steaks for Spudbug and Major Junction.

"**What are you going to eat, Fabian?**" asked Spudbug, sawing into the meat. "**Steak, like us?**"

"**Um,**" muttered Fabian uneasily.

"**Have some lentils. They are delicious and good for you,**" suggested Simon.

"**Wait a minute – if you eat what they're**

eating then I'm going to think you have a deal with them," said Spudbug.

"But you just suggested he eat steak! Do *you* have a deal with him?"

"Steak, Fabian. Eat steak."

"Lentils."

"Steak."

Simon said nothing for a moment then very quietly muttered, "**Lentils.**"

Spudbug slammed down her knife and the glasses on the table jumped. "**You are so annoying! I know exactly what you're up to!**"

"Really?" said Simon, smiling sweetly. "I didn't think you Spams knew much about anything at all."

"I know I'll tear you into little—"

"May I interrupt?" asked Frank. He felt someone needed to get a hold of this situation which was spiralling out of control. It looked as though this whole day might fail before it even properly began.

Simon and Spudbug looked at him.

"King Fabian is too polite to say so, but I'm afraid he won't be able to have either the steak or the lentils."

"Won't he?" asked Spudbug.

"Won't I?" asked Fabian.

"Why not?" demanded Simon.

"Good question," said Frank. "A very fine question. He won't be eating *anything* today, because today ... is the Feast of Rodney Longshanks."

"Rodney Longshanks?" asked Simon.

"Who's that?" said Spudbug.

"Rodney who?" asked Fabian – rather unhelpfully, thought Frank. He was beginning to think that the king wasn't quite as smart as he had thought a king might be.

"Yes, Rodney Longshanks. You will remember him, Your Majesty, as one of the most revered and celebrated Gabslandians ever," continued Frank. "He was a simple man from the east of the country with an incredible story."

"What is it?" asked Spudbug.

"What is it?" Frank swallowed. "What's his story?" He hadn't expected to have to come up with a story.

"Yes, what is it?" said Spudbug, menacingly. "Tell us. And it better be good."

Frank looked around the table. Ella gave him an encouraging smile.

"Oh, it is good," said Frank. "You see, Rodney Longshanks was involved in an extraordinary relationship. With a shark."

"A shark?"

"A shark. He first came across it when he was a small boy – this was over a hundred years ago. The story goes that he was swimming in shallow waters when his younger sister was pulled under by a great white. Rodney Longshanks dived down, swam up to the shark and bit him on the nose. The shark opened its mouth, releasing Rodney's sister and swam away. His sister was fine, by the way – except for a sore leg. Amazing, yes. But not as amazing as what happened years later.

"Rodney, now in his twenties, was diving for pearls in the ocean and he got into trouble. He hadn't realized how far out he had swum and was tired and a long way from the shore. It was at that moment a shark appeared in front of him. A shark with a bit of its nose missing! The same shark! The shark swam towards him at speed. Rodney was too exhausted to fight back this time so he decided to try a different tactic and to communicate with the shark instead. He began to sing a sad song about his sister's sore leg and how he forgave the shark, how he understood that we all need to eat, how we are all only acting in the best interests of ourselves and of our families and

how everyone can change. The shark was so moved by the song that it didn't eat Rodney and instead carried him to shore on its back.

"Since that day there has never been a shark attack in Gabsland. We celebrate that each year on Rodney Longshanks Day – by not eating breakfast, the way the shark didn't eat Rodney Longshanks."

There was a pause.

"Beautiful," murmured Simon.

"Amazing," said Fabian, wondering why he had never heard this famous Gabslandian tale before.

Spudbug took a slurp of her dishwater. "Rubbish. A shark is a killing machine, not some sort of soppy berk. And, remind me – how much coast is there around Gabsland? That's right – none! The country is surrounded by land on all sides. Of course there hasn't been a shark attack in Gabsland, there's no sea!"

Frank flushed with embarrassment. He was a bit annoyed with himself – he came up with dozens of better stories than this every single day in the kitchen.

"Are we being ... lied to?" asked Simon, holding a hand to his cheek. "Lying is a breach of trust. Without trust we have nothing."

Princess Ella spoke up. "He's not lying. Yes it does sound ridiculous, I agree. But the fact is it's true! Supreme Leader Spudbug, you are quite right to point out there are no oceans around the coast of Gabsland. Frank has indeed got a little confused there. The incident happened in the warm oceans to the south of Gabsland. What I believe Frank meant to say was that no Gabslandian has been injured by a shark anywhere in the *world* since Rodney Longshanks sang to that shark."

"Yes, that's what I meant!" said Frank. "You must forgive me for getting confused! Can I fetch you some more dishwater, Supreme Leader?"

Spudbug gave him a long look. "You a liar, boy? I suspect you might be. Now, when is the inspection of the troops?" she asked, peering suspiciously at the day's programme of events. "That's the bit I'm most interested in. See this famous army of yours."

"Half an hour, Your Supremeness," said Frank, looking at his schedule.

Spudbug drained the last of her drink and

then she and Major Junction walked to the door.

"**Got my eye on you, lad,**" she said to Frank and marched out.

Simon and Googie stood up.

"**Thank you for breakfast,**" Simon said, with a pained expression. "**I am sorry that our hug was rejected, though. Not a good start. This feels ominous, Fabian. We always try to stay optimistic, but...**"

Googie nodded, Simon shook his head sadly and they turned on their heels and left.

Princess Ella rushed to the door to make sure they had gone, then turned to Frank.

"**The Feast of Rodney Longshanks?**" She looked as though she wasn't sure whether to laugh or tell him off. "**What the...?**"

"**I could see the king was in an awkward**

133

spot!" Frank protested. "And I figured he didn't want to drink dishwater, so..."

"That's true. You did well to intervene," said Fabian. "I wish I *could* eat something," he added wistfully. "But it's the Feast of Rodney Longshanks, and we must honour him."

Frank blinked. "But ... I just made it up..."

Fabian was already heading out of the door. "I'm off to get dressed for the inspection," he called. "Doing brilliantly, Dimmock!"

Frank sighed. He and Ella looked at each other.

"We need to raise our game," said Ella at last. "It's very important that the inspection of the troops goes well. Can I count on you?"

"Of course," said Frank firmly, trying to sound confident. He badly wanted to help pull this off, but he couldn't help feeling that he was dangerously out of his depth.

"Thank you," said Ella, hoping that her own unease wasn't too obvious.

CHAPTER TWELVE

According to Dimmock's itinerary, there was half an hour before the inspection of the troops. Frank escorted the queen into her night chamber. A specially fitted room in which all the windows were blacked out so that it was completely dark. Queen Charlotte liked to lie there and imagine she was at her own funeral and everyone was sharing memories about how wonderful she was. That made her feel all warm inside.

The queen liked to spend a good hour a day doing this.

Then, Frank ran down to the kitchen.

"Well?" asked Cook.

"It's so difficult!" said Frank. "The Spams are frightening, the Hipneys are fussy, and the king... Well ... he's less ... in control than I was expecting."

"Our king is a hero and a genius."

"Yes, of course. He's just a hero and a genius in a slightly different way to how I imagined. Ella is all right but she can be a bit critical. I'm just a kitchen boy; this is ridiculous."

"Yes, you are the kitchen boy." The cook tossed a washcloth at Frank. "Time to do the washing-up from breakfast. As my old uncle used to say, 'You can't have your washing up and eat it.'"

"What?! I'm due out on the parade ground in half an hour."

"That's long enough to do the washing-up. Put on your apron. Get on with it!"

*

After finishing the washing-up in record speed, Frank grabbed his jacket and ran out to the parade ground. He had wanted to visit the dungeon to try and get some advice from Dimmock but there hadn't been time.

Still, the inspection of the troops should be easy, he thought. He just had to stand at the side while Fabian rode his horse up and down the lines of soldiers. It was an excuse to show off the smart uniforms the soldiers wore and how good they were at marching about. Frank was looking forward to it; he had never been allowed on the parade ground when it was happening.

The parade ground was around the back of the palace. Surrounded on three sides by trees which were all covered in blossom, was the square piece of ground on which the soldiers had already gathered, standing in three neat lines. The fourth side of the parade ground led down to the edge of the lake. It was a pretty spot, especially on a sunny day like today.

Two tents had been set up: one for the Spams, the other for the Hipneys. Dimmock had arranged this and, to his relief, Frank saw that the Spams had several urns of dishwater and bowls of stale crusts laid out, while the Hipneys had a vat of mushroom soup.

Frank smoothed down his enormous uniform as Supreme Leader Spudbug, Major Junction and the other six members of the Spam delegation arrived.

"Those Hipneys are late again, I see," said Spudbug, glancing at her watch. "It's ill-disciplined and rude. We are always four minutes early for everything."

"Two hundred and forty seconds," murmured Major Junction under his breath, who knew what was coming.

"Two hundred and forty seconds!" bellowed Spudbug. "That right, Junction?"

Major Junction, who occasionally quite fancied a lie-in, nodded. "Absolutely."

"Well, please follow me," said Frank. "Your viewing tent is just here."

They took their places.

"**Will there be guns fired?**" asked Spudbug.

"**Not to my knowledge, Your Supreme Leaderness,**" said Frank.

"Cannons?"

"I don't think so."

"Bombs?"

"I doubt there'll be bombs."

"Any explosions at all?"

"No, Supreme Leader Spudbug."

"**BORING!!**" shouted Spudbug and all the Spams laughed uproariously, "**BOOOOOOORRRRRRIIIINNNGGG!**"

"**Is that because today's the Feast of Rodney Lounge Slacks?**" boomed Major Junction to more hilarity.

Frank smiled as calmly as he could, poured them each a glass of dishwater juice and ran over to the Hipneys who were just arriving.

"What are they yelling about?" asked Simon. "It's a terrible noise and, frankly, uncouth."

"Not entirely sure, sir," said Frank.

"They don't seem to be taking this seriously. Is that a good sign or a bad sign do you think, No Better Than Me?"

"I wouldn't want to comment without a proper period of consultation and reflection," Googie said.

"Fair enough," Simon said. "Show us to our seats, please. I hope there will be no guns or explosions today. I have a bit of a headache coming on."

Frank settled them in and handed out some raw carrots. Then he noticed King Fabian wandering across the parade ground looking lost.

"Ah, there you are, dear fellow. Have you

143

seen ... one of those things? Four legs, long face."

"Your horse, Your Majesty?"

"That's it! Or do I mean a dog?"

"I think you mean a horse, Your Majesty. When did you last see it?"

"How am I supposed to remember that?" The king blinked at Frank. "Do I know you?"

Frank stared at the king. There was a faraway look in the king's eyes. He was also unsteady on his feet and seemed to be acting even odder and more absent-mindedly than earlier. This was bad. This was *very* bad. Was this because the king had missed breakfast? Or was it sunstroke?

Get him on the horse, thought Frank. *Once he's on the horse it'll all come back to him.*

"Perhaps you would like to sit in the shade while I find your horse, Your Majesty?"

Frank linked arms with the king and led him towards the stables. Princess Ella saw them and ran over.

"What's going on?"

"It's your father," said Frank. "He's a little bit..."

"A sheaf of straw for the night!" yelled Fabian.

Ella frowned. "I see. He does go a bit to pieces if he hasn't eaten. You and your shark story! Dimmock would never have let this happen. You go and get some food and I'll put him on his horse."

*

Frank ran into the kitchen. "I need a snack for the king! Quick!" He grabbed an apple and ran out again.

Knowing that they were keeping the Spams

and the Hipneys waiting, Ella wasted no time in getting the king on to his horse and they were already back at the parade ground by the time Frank arrived.

"An apple, Your Majesty!" Frank said and handed the bemused king the fruit.

King Fabian looked curiously at the apple as though he had never seen one before in his life.

"What ... is ... this?" he asked slowly.

"An apple, Your Majesty," repeated Frank.

"What's it for?"

"Eating?"

"What?"

"Eating."

"Put it in your mouth and eat it," snapped Ella impatiently. "I'm going to tell the other leaders that you are coming over now."

And she stomped off.

"My mouth," said Fabian. He lifted the apple and smacked himself on the forehead with it. **"Mouth?"**

His horse, wondering what was taking so long, swung its head around to see what was going on.

"Mouth!" said the king when he saw the horse's face. **"Mouth!"**

Fabian leaned forwards and shoved the apple into his horse's mouth.

The horse chomped on it a few times and swallowed.

"Mouth," said King Fabian, then slumped forward and fell asleep, arms around his horse's neck.

Frank gasped. This was awful.

Ella came running back.

"What's happening? He's supposed to be inspecting the troops!"

"He's asleep," hissed Frank. "What are we going to do?"

Ella thought for a minute. "Let's put him in the stable to sleep. We can't keep the leaders waiting any longer. It's really important that we show we can stick to the schedule."

"OK, we put him in the stable. Then what?"

"Then you're going to get on a horse and inspect the troops."

"I'm sorry – what?" said Frank. "Me?"

"You. It'll leave me free to talk to the leaders and keep things running smoothly."

"I can't inspect the troops!"

"You have to. And you owe me one, remember? So you're doing it."

"But!"

"No buts. Let's go."

They led Fabian to the stable and, as gently as they could, dragged him off his horse. They tried to make him as comfortable as possible using straw as a pillow, then left, locking the stable door behind them.

"The last thing we need is him wandering around, spouting rubbish at the wrong moment," said the princess. "Right, get on that one." She pointed at an enormous grey horse in the next-door stable. "He's already saddled up. I'll help you."

The horse was so big they had to fetch a ladder and prop it up against the animal so Frank could climb up. He heaved himself on to the saddle.

"Oh, I am so high up!" he said. "This is ridiculous."

"Just imagine you are a medieval knight

about to go into battle!" suggested Ella. "And it really is a battle – a battle for the future of our country. No pressure!"

Once she had adjusted the stirrups and Frank gave a nod, she led the horse out of the stables and over to the parade ground.

Frank had never ridden a horse before but

had taken Ella's advice and was now, in his mind, a brave and noble knight leading his troops to fight a dangerous enemy. Possibly a fire-breathing dragon.

"We do this for our country, our families and our pets," he muttered to himself. "Let us be courageous, let us be intrepid and let us be alive when it is over. That's the main thing."

"What are you muttering about?" Ella asked him.

"Nothing," he said.

They had reached the parade ground.

"Right, this is it," said Ella. "Good luck, Sir Frank."

"One last thing – what is this horse called?" asked Frank.

"Cheeseballs," said Ella. "I know, silly name for such a magnificent horse. Well, good luck!"

She slapped Cheeseballs so hard on the bottom that the startled animal reared up on its back legs, lifting its front legs high off the ground and nearly throwing Frank off. Somehow, Frank managed to grab the reins with one hand and the horse's mane with the other and just about stopped himself from being launched backwards on to the hard ground.

The huge animal kicked its front legs a couple of times and Frank worried that the beast was going to fall over backwards. Frank wasn't entirely sure what happened when a big horse landed on top of you, but he was willing to bet it wasn't much fun.

Finally, after a moment or two of sheer terror on Frank's part and lots of snorting on the horse's, Cheeseballs dropped back on to all fours with Frank's arms tightly around its neck.

Frank had no time to be relieved, though, as the horse took off, bolting towards the parade ground at incredible speed. Frank clung on as if his life depended on it. Which, in fact, it did.

Frank tried desperately to think if he knew anything about horses that might help in a situation like this and, remembering that reins were the things which helped you to control a horse, Frank grabbed them in both hands and pulled as hard as he could. Luckily, the horse obeyed, screeching to a halt right in the middle of the parade ground, in front of the assembled troops, his big head twisting and turning, his eyes wild and huge dollops of spit flying out of his mouth in all directions.

Frank shouted "**CHEESEBALLS!**" at the top of his voice, but it was a bit late for that because the horse had already stopped.

"**Is he shouting 'cheeseballs'?**" asked Spudbug.

Simon nodded. "**I think so,**" he said. "**Totally normal, aren't they, these Gabslandians?**"

Spudbug gave a snort of laughter, then remembered that Simon was her mortal enemy and narrowed her eyes instead.

Frank looked around. Three rows of soldiers with twelve soldiers in each row, were trying very hard to remain professional and to stare directly ahead as they were supposed to and not to look at the thing they all desperately wanted to look at, which was the boy on the horse that he clearly couldn't handle, shouting "**CHEESEBALLS**". Some of the soldiers couldn't resist though and were watching Frank out of the corner of their eyes.

"EYES FORWARD!" yelled the Sergeant Major.

"CHEESEBALLS!" shouted Frank again for no apparent reason. "Good morning!" he said as calmly as he could manage, which wasn't very calmly at all because he was shaking like a leaf. "This year, today being the Feast of Roman Tony Planks..."

"You mean Rodney Longshanks?" yelled Ella.

"That's what I said," said Frank, "Rodney Purple Pants..."

"Rodney Longshanks!"

"Rodney Longshanks, yes, thank you. So, listen, our gracious King Fabian is dealing with emergency affairs of state and as a result, I,

Frank, will be inspecting the troops instead of the king."

"Boo!" shouted Spudbug.

"Keep that horse spit away from us!" shouted Simon. "We're allergic."

"Yes, I shall inspect our troops," said Frank, wondering whether you inspected troops from on top of a horse or by walking on the ground. Frank was inadvertently pulling the reins to the right and consequently the horse suddenly lurched three steps sideways.

"CHEESEBALLS!" shouted Frank again.

"Why does he keep shouting 'cheeseballs'?" said Spudbug. "Is it a kingdom-of-Gabsland tradition?"

"No idea," said Simon. "They sound disgusting."

"It's making me hungry," said Spudbug. "Don't suppose you have any cheeseballs on you, Junction?"

"I do not."

"Shame."

"I will now inspect the troops," said Frank.

"So you keep saying," said Simon.

"Get on with it!" shouted Spudbug. "I want to hear some gunfire."

Frank decided there was no way he could drive the horse along the rows of soldiers without causing mayhem (*do you "drive" a horse?* he wondered) so decided to dismount. Which was easier said than done.

Muttering "good boy" to the horse, he pulled his feet out of the stirrups and swung his left leg over the back end of the horse. He was balanced on his stomach, legs hanging off one side, head hanging over the other. Now this was the tricky bit. He had to wriggle backwards until he slid off the horse and try to land on his feet. If he fell over that would be a bad look.

He started to push himself backwards, but he could barely make any progress. Something he was wearing must have snagged on something on Cheeseball's saddle. He jerked back and forth a couple of times but no luck. He was stuck.

Unfortunately, Ella was behind him so he couldn't give her a signal that he needed help. He was facing the soldiers, many of whom were again having a great deal of difficulty keeping their gaze forward and not watching all this drama unfolding.

Frank was just about to call out when Cheeseballs started to walk very slowly along the front line of troops. *Of course!* thought

Frank. *Cheeseballs has probably done this inspection before and knows what to do.* As he was facing the line of troops he thought he'd style it out and inspect them. **"Very shiny boots, excellent,"** he said to the first soldier. **"Nice shirt,"** to the next, as Cheeseballs carried him along the line.

"Why is he hanging half off that horse?" asked Spudbug.

"No idea," said Major Junction.

"Great hair," said Frank to another soldier. "Looking good."

Once they got to the end of the row, Cheeseballs rounded the final soldier and began to walk along the second row. Unfortunately, this meant that Frank was now facing the wrong way. He was facing away from the second row of soldiers and looking instead at the backs of the troops in the first row. The troops he'd just inspected.

There was nothing for it but to keep going.

"Great heels, well-polished," he said to the first. "Clean neck," he said to the second.

"Why is he inspecting the backs of those soldiers?" asked Spudbug.

"No idea," said Major Junction.

"Because he's very thorough!" called out Ella.

Frank stuck to it even though it wasn't at all comfortable dangling from Cheeseballs in this way. "Bit of dandruff there, soldier. You have clean elbows. Good to see you washing behind your ears."

Once Cheeseballs had walked along the final row, he didn't stop but kept walking in the direction of the stables.

"Thanks for coming! Inspection over!" shouted Frank before he disappeared round the corner.

Spudbug and Simon looked at each other. Spudbug's lips twitched. Simon swallowed. And then they both burst out laughing.

Meanwhile, in the stable, King Fabian

woke up, saw his horse doing a huge poo
and screamed.

CHAPTER THIRTEEN

Ella and Frank managed to get the king back into his bedroom without any further ado. Frank brought some soup and bread up from the kitchen and Fabian ate it hungrily.

"Dad, you don't need to bite the spoon when you're eating soup!"

Fabian nodded meekly and put down the spoon. "I feel peculiar, Ella," he said. "Why was I asleep next to a pooing horse? What happened?"

"You were acting very strangely," said Ella.

"I don't remember a thing," said Fabian. "Most odd."

"We don't have long before the next event," said Frank, scanning the itinerary anxiously.

"What is it?" asked the king.

"The acrobats."

"Oh, that's good news. We just have to sit there. I'd better get changed; these clothes are filthy from lying in that stable."

Frank handed him a clean shirt. "Might be a good idea to wear the necklace the Spams gave you. Show a bit of willing."

"Good idea! Unwrap it for me, will you?" He threw the unopened present to Frank.

"We must show those neighbours of ours that they have nothing to fear," said the king. "That I am a strong, competent and reliable ruler."

"You've got your shirt on back to front, sire."

"So I have."

*

Ella knocked on the door of Queen Charlotte's night chamber. It was time, she thought, to enlist her mother's help.

"Go away. I'm dead."

"No, you're not," Ella said patiently.

"I almost am."

"Not even close. We need you to join us."

"In the sunshine?!"

"Yes. It's the acrobatics."

There was a silence inside the room. Ella rested her forehead against the door.

"Mum?" she said at last. "It's **really**

important that today goes well. Otherwise Hipnia and Spamon might think it's OK to call in their debts. And that would be our worst nightmare. Dad isn't ... well, he isn't the most impressive in this sort of situation. In fact, he seems even weirder than usual. Dimmock is in a cell. The new Dimmock doesn't really know what he's doing, and—" Ella suddenly felt overcome. "I need your help, Mum."

Another silence.

"Ugh. I'll need to put sunscreen on. And a hat. And find a parasol."

There was nothing Queen Charlotte disliked more than getting even the faintest tan.

"All that leaping about. It's so energetic and unnecessary. But, yes, I'll come."

Ella breathed a sigh of relief, but there was no time to lose.

"Hurry up!"

"I'll try! I'm half-dead remember."

＊

Frank left the king putting on his socks and ran down to the kitchen.

"Where have you been?" asked Cook.

"Inspecting the troops."

"Don't be daft," she retorted. "You! Inspecting the troops! I'll inspect you in a minute. I need those onions peeled and chopped."

"But I have to get back out there and entertain the other leaders."

"I'll entertain you in a minute," said Cook.

"Cheeky beggar! As my old uncle used to say, 'You can take an onion to water but you can't make it drink.'"

"What?"

"Get chopping!"

"Seriously…"

"I'll seriously you in a minute. Listen, self-peeling onions haven't been invented yet and I have enough to deal with trying to cook for so many people with no help. Peel them before I peel you!"

Frank sighed. It was probably quicker to do as she asked.

CHAPTER FOURTEEN

Ella was the first to arrive at the rose garden, where the acrobatics display was due to be held. She could see the Spams. Spudbug had rolled up a large towel and she was flicking the others with it while they winced and pretended to be enjoying themselves.

The Hipneys sat cross-legged close by, trying to do group meditation. Simon was leading it but Googie kept interrupting.

"Let us face the day with an open heart,"

said Simon.

"Do we want them to be 'open'?" said Googie. "Our hearts?"

Simon gritted his teeth. "What sort of heart would you like to have?" he asked as politely as he could manage.

"A serene one?"

Simon said perhaps they could look to face the day with both a serene *and* an open heart and would they like to have a group hug? So they did. Simon was pleased with himself for being the bigger person and not getting into an argument about what sort of hearts they should have. Googie was annoyed she hadn't come up with the idea of a group hug first and fought to keep a serene heart.

Ella called everyone over and seated them in front of a marked-out grassy area by the pond where the acrobatics display was soon to happen.

"Where's Fabian?" asked Spudbug. "Can he not make it because it's the Feast of Bernard Bad Breath or something?"

The Spams laughed. Simon surprised himself by laughing too. Googie shot him a look and he sobered.

"They're terrible brutes," murmured Googie.

"Terrible," agreed Simon. "But sometimes they're quite funny."

"King Fabian is just on his way," said Ella. "He's just been re-arranging his trophies for military prowess and diplomacy," she added, pointedly.

King Fabian and Queen Charlotte strode across the lawn. Fabian had his shirt open to the waist with the necklace given to him by the

Spams around his neck. Hanging from it was a big golden orb, the bottom of which was resting lightly on the top of Fabian's little pot belly. Fabian was not a hairy man – he had maybe ten or twelve wiry hairs growing out of his chest – but, as he walked, the necklace swung gently from side to side, catching the chest hairs and causing him some discomfort.

The queen was a vision in white. She had on a long, flowing, white dress; white gloves; a large white wide-brimmed hat; a white veil; white sunglasses and a huge white parasol.

"Well, isn't this marvellous?" said Fabian as he sat down. "A beautiful day and some world-class acrobatics to look forward to. What could be better?"

"Glad you could make it," said Spudbug. "Happy Feast of Rowdy Trousers!"

"Thank you!" said Fabian.

"I see you are wearing our gift," said Spudbug.

"Yes, it's marvellous. Marvellous. A new look for me, but I think wearing it with an open-neck shirt gives it a certain something."

"Oh, it gives it something, certainly," said Spudbug. "How are you, Queen Charlotte? That is you under all that, isn't it?"

"Hello," said Queen Charlotte, barely audibly.

Spudbug waited for her to say something else but nothing was forthcoming.

"May I fetch you something to drink, my love?" Fabian asked his wife.

There was a murmur from underneath all the white cloth.

"Sorry, what?" Fabian asked.

"Water," came the soft reply.

Fabian looked around for Dimmock but he was nowhere to be seen. *That's not like him,* thought the king.

"Ella, please fetch your mother some water."

Ella collected a glass of water from a tray.

"I understand that the kingdom of Gabsland is world-renowned for its acrobats," said Simon earnestly. "Please, do tell us more, King Fabian."

"We train them from childhood. Any child that shows an interest in tumbling, we send them to acrobatic school. Gabsland has been celebrated for its world-class acrobats for centuries. My father was an accomplished acrobat himself."

"Really?"

"Yes, he could do somersaults, back flips, the splits, all sorts." Fabian's face fell. "I couldn't, though. I can't even touch my toes."

Ella pressed the glass into her mother's gloved hand.

"So you didn't inherit your father's physical

skills but you did inherit his vast wealth and unfettered power," said Simon, a little tartly.

"Ha, I certainly did!" said Fabian.

The queen realized she'd have to lift her veil to drink the water. She felt for the bottom of it with a gloved hand.

Fabian continued, "I can't wait to show you our world-class athletes. Excellent, if you like this sort of thing." He looked wistful. "Although, my absolute favourite hobby is making daisy chains."

The queen couldn't locate the bottom of the veil so she threw the glass over her shoulder to get rid of it.

Major Junction marched over from the topiary gardens.

"Sorry I'm late," he called. Spudbug glared at him – lack of punctuality was most displeasing. "Hope I haven't missed anything?"

"Just starting. Pull up a chair, take the world off your feet," said Fabian.

Frank, finished with the onions, had run as fast as he could across the lawn to join the others. His eyes always reacted badly to chopping onions and he had tears streaming down his face.

"Will there be punching in this show?" asked Spudbug eagerly.

"Not unless acrobatics has changed dramatically in the last few years," said Fabian.

"Shame," said Spudbug. "You Gabslandians are soft, know that?"

"That's not true at all!" protested Fabian. "We are a warrior nation. A tough nation. A fighting nation. I say, would you mind moving your foot? You're standing on my ruched satin slipperettes."

Frank panted over, wiping his cheeks.

"Are you crying?" Spudbug asked him.

"A bit," said Frank. "It's the excitement. Can't wait to see these amazing acrobats."

"Ladies and gentlemen!" announced Ella. "Please put your hands together for the Gabsland Acrobatic Display Team!"

Two acrobats ran across the lawn, each pulling a covered wagon behind them. Each wagon had a low black canvas roof on which another acrobat was doing a handstand on the feet of another acrobat doing a handstand. Remarkably they all managed to keep their balance as the wagons bumped and jiggled across the lawn.

The wagons were brought to a stop facing the watching dignitaries, the handstand acrobats swayed as it did so but kept upright.

"Not bad," said Spudbug grudgingly.

At a signal, all the acrobats jumped down

and stood as the audience applauded. Each had one letter on the front of their outfits and standing in a row they spelled out **"TUMBLE"**.

The smallest one, the **"M"**, grabbed an empty barrel from the wagon, turned it on its side so that it could roll back and forth, placed a plank on it and jumped up, rocking from side to side, skilfully

keeping his balance. Everyone applauded.

Three acrobats, "T", "U" and "E" stood facing away from one another and, putting all their weight on to one leg, each lifted their other leg high in the air behind them so that they were touching. That was impressive as they were practically doing the splits.

A fourth acrobat, "B", jumped up and did a headstand on the three high feet. A fifth acrobat, "L", climbed up and did a handstand on top of the fourth acrobat. Everyone applauded. The acrobats disentangled and formed a line to accept more applause.

"Hey, you're spelling out BUMLET!" observed Spudbug. "Is that a small bottom?!"

The Spams were delighted. The Hipneys tried to maintain serene and open hearts.

The acrobats, smiling broadly with their mouths if not their eyes, broke up the line and, fetching a variety of barrels, began to pile them on top of each other into a wobbly tower.

"That's very impressive," shouted King Fabian and everyone applauded.

"Your father seems to be doing all right," said Frank to Ella.

"He's keeping it together, I suppose," said Ella. "For now."

The small acrobat leapt down and dismantled the wobbly tower while three others performed another stunt. The biggest acrobat stood with his legs wide apart. Another climbed up his back, stood on his shoulders and, hands palm to palm, did a handstand on the first's outstretched arms. The audience could see how hard they were both having to work, they were shaking with the effort. Then, a third climbed up and he did a handstand on the second acrobat's upside-down feet.

"Whoa! That's not bad at all. Maybe you lot are not as soft as you look, Fabian," said Spudbug.

Fabian did not reply; he was distracted. He frantically flapped his arms at the air in front of him.

The three acrobats disengaged and lined up to bow.

"Now you spell BUM!" howled Spudbug. The Spams fell about.

Fabian's hand flicking was becoming more intense and Ella and Frank looked at each other.

"I'm going over," said Ella. **"Something's up."**

The acrobats were building a human pyramid. Three of them in a row on all fours, two acrobats balancing on their knees on those three, and one acrobat standing on top of them.

"Ladies and gentlemen! We need a volunteer!" said the highest acrobat.

"Simon?" asked Fabian, still pawing at the empty air in front of him. **"Fancy being the star of the show?"**

"Let me check, Fabian," said Simon. **"It goes

against the Hipney ethos to be the star of anything."

The Hipneys went into a huddle.

"Come on, you lot," shouted Spudbug. "We haven't got all day. You going to volunteer, or what?"

Simon broke away from the group.

"Do you mind, Spudbug?" he said. "We're just voting."

"You WHAT?" boomed Spudbug. "How about a simple 'yes' or 'no'?"

"If only it were that simple," said Simon.

"It is that simple, man," said Spudbug. "Look, I'll do it! Or you do it! Or else!"

"Is that a threat?"

"You wish."

"No, you wish."

"No, you wish."

"No, you wish."

"No, you wish."

"STOP!" shouted Ella. Spudbug and Simon turned to look at her. "Shall I do it?" she suggested. "Shall I help the acrobats and we can all get back to having a lovely time?"

"Fine by me," said Spudbug, glowering at Simon.

"Simon?" asked Ella. "Good for you?"

"Don't ask *him*," Spudbug said. "He'll need to check with his committee."

"Yes, Princess Ella," said Simon defiantly. "That works for us."

"Um, Simon," ventured Googie. "You really ought to confer with the executive before..."

"I said it's fine," said Simon tensely. "So it's fine."

"Oooh, someone's acting like a leader for a

change," mocked Spudbug.

"**Great!**" jumped in Ella before they started arguing again. "**I'll do it. Oi,**" she hissed at Frank. "**Keep an eye on the king.**"

Fabian had now got up out of his chair and was not only batting away at the empty space in front of him but running in circles grabbing frantically at the back of his trousers.

"**Is he all right?**" asked Spudbug, pointing at Fabian.

"**Oh, fine,**" said Ella breezily, and she ran over to the acrobats. She figured the quicker she helped the acrobats do this trick, the quicker they could get Fabian back to the palace. "**What do you want me to do?**" she asked them.

The acrobats had placed a long plank of wood

187

over a barrel in front of the human pyramid. The acrobat explained that the plank was balanced like a seesaw. Ella was to stand at the end on the ground, then the acrobat from the top of the pyramid would jump down on to the other end of the plank, sending Ella shooting up into the air and on to the top of the human pyramid.

"Wow," said Ella. "That's ... well ... are you sure?"

Fabian was running up and down shouting, "They're eating me! They're eating me!"

"I'll do it," said Ella quickly. "Let's go!" She walked over and stood on the end of the plank. "Right, I'm ready!"

The acrobat climbed back up to the top of the pyramid.

Frank sprinted over to Fabian. "Are you all right, Your Majesty?"

Fabian grabbed Frank by the collar and pulled him face to face. **"They. Are. Eating. Me,"** he said.

"I see," said Frank. He glanced around to see the major and Googie watching them closely. He lowered his voice. **"Shall we watch Ella do her trick and then get you into the palace and we can stop them ... whatever they are ... from eating you?"**

"No! Now!"

Frank was aware that they were being watched by the others. So he laughed out loud and said, **"Good one, Your Majesty!"** as if the king was making a joke.

"Here we go!" said Ella. **"Go for it, I'm ready!"**

The acrobat focused intently on the plank. He had to judge the angle of his jump to perfection to send Ella into the air in the right direction. He took a couple of deep breaths.

Googie gasped. **"Wait! Is that an ant under the plank?"**

The acrobat bent his knees in preparation to jump.

"It is! It's an ant! Simon! It'll get squashed!"

The acrobat leapt into the air.

Simon scrambled forward to try and rescue the ant that was in danger.

Fabian, screaming now, threw himself on to the ground, writhing in agony and scratching at his back, legs and chest.

"They're everywhere!"

The acrobat fell through the air towards the landing spot.

Simon threw himself at the plank.

Ella held her breath. Frank held his breath. The queen had been holding her breath for about a minute anyway.

Simon stumbled and staggered, out of control, towards the spot the acrobat was aiming for.

"DON'T CRUSH THAT ANT!!" he bellowed.

The acrobat and Simon both hit the end of the plank at the same time, generating way more force on it than was required, slamming it into the ground and sending Ella careering high into the air, over the human pyramid, over the bushes, until she fell face-first into the pond beyond.

There was mayhem.

The Hipneys rushed forward to see if the ant had been harmed and formed a protective circle around it. The Spams howled with laughter. Fabian howled with pain. The acrobats collapsed in a big pile. The queen didn't move a muscle.

Frank rushed over to see if Ella was hurt. Luckily, the pond was deep and Ella was an excellent swimmer so, apart from being soaking wet, she was fine.

"Get the king inside!" she told Frank, as he helped her out of the pond.

"But you're soaking wet."

"I'll be fine. Just get him inside and find out what's wrong with him." She wrung out her hair. "Something weird is going on. Dad is weird but he isn't usually *this* weird. We need to talk to Dimmock. He's the only one around here with any sense."

Frank ran to Fabian and dragged him to his feet. "I can help, Your Majesty. Come with me!" Frank grabbed the king's hands and pulled him across the garden and into the palace.

Being a butler is a lot harder than peeling onions, he thought.

CHAPTER FIFTEEN

Frank dragged King Fabian into the kitchen; its door was the nearest to the garden.

Cook was sitting in her chair by the fireplace, left foot in a bowl of warm water, removing dead skin from her right foot with a pumice stone. This was not something she should have been doing in the kitchen but in the privacy of her bedroom. The lunch was cooked and ready and she had found herself, unusually, with a spare fifteen minutes. She had been hoping to give her feet a going over before Frank came back but she had never in her wildest imaginings thought that the king would come in.

The king had never visited the kitchen and, on the rare occasions they had met in the sixteen years she had worked there, she had only ever had the briefest of conversations with him. So when the king ran into the kitchen, she panicked. She threw the pumice stone into the fire; she threw the bowl of water into the fire too. Then she picked up the chair she had been sitting on and threw that into the fire as well.

She needn't have bothered. The king was completely unaware of anything but his own pain.

"Where does it hurt?" Frank asked him.

"Everywhere!" the king wailed. He started

tearing at his clothes. He grabbed the orb hanging around his neck and wrenched it off. Then came the rest: his jacket, ripping every button from his shirt as he tore it off; down came the trousers, removing shoes and socks at the same time. His vest and pants too. In no time he was naked and frenziedly brushing his hands across his body.

Cook blinked. This was all very unexpected.

"Are they gone?" he asked Frank.

"Are what gone, Your Majesty?" said Frank, shielding his eyes.

"The things, the biters, the creatures that are doing this to me!" screeched Fabian. **"Look!"**

Frank peeked through his fingers. The king was indeed covered in dozens of little red marks and they looked painful.

"Look, there's one!" Fabian slapped his hand on the floor and lifted his palm to inspect it. A small dead red insect stuck to his sweaty skin.

An ant.

"Here, Your Majesty," said Cook, offering him a tea towel. "I thought you might like to cover up your ... um ... crown jewels."

"Oh, yes," said the king, now aware of his nakedness. He had calmed down a little. He took the tea towel, which was illustrated with pictures of baby hedgehogs, and covered himself up.

"Now, let's have a look at that creature, please, Your Majesty."

Cook took the insect over to

the window where it was lighter.

"Goodness," she said. "This is a red fire ant. How extraordinary!"

"What's a red fire ant?" asked Frank, examining it.

"A red fire ant is a nasty little beggar. Vicious sting, as you have discovered, Your Majesty. Horrible creatures, extremely painful. I will get some ointment and an ice pack. Those bites will swell up and blister. We need to give you a wash first. Get the bathtub out, Frank, and fill it with nice warm soapy water. We'll sort you out in no time, sir."

Frank was still frowning at the squished insect. "But where did it come from?"

"That is a good question. You don't get red fire ants in Gabsland. Careful, Frank, there may be more!"

Frank dropped the king's clothes that he'd been gathering and examined his arms anxiously. He stepped back and his foot kicked against something: the necklace's golden orb. He gingerly bent down to pick it up. It was hollow. Frank turned it over in his hands and was about to hand it to the king when he spotted a tiny hole near the bottom. A hole possibly just big enough for a fire ant to escape through.

Could the insects have been hiding inside the orb and scrambled out while the king was watching the acrobatics? How had they got there? Turning the orb and examining the rest of it, Frank found another tiny hole near the top.

Frank was puzzled. One tiny hole could have been a flaw from when they made the orb but two…? That felt deliberate. But if you were hiding ants in a globe, how would you get them inside? Frank tried twisting the orb; nothing happened. He tried twisting it the other way and it began to unscrew.

"It's a secret compartment!"

Cook and the king came over.

"Look!"

Frank prised the circular lid off and two red fire ants came scuttling out. He dropped the orb in shock. Cook's big calloused right foot came down hard, squashing both ants in one go.

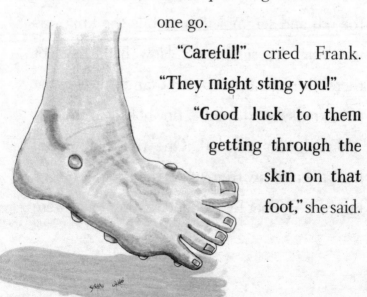

"Careful!" cried Frank. "They might sting you!"

"Good luck to them getting through the skin on that foot," she said.

"Hardest substance known to man, the skin on my feet. As my old uncle used to say: 'You were born with a hard silver foot in your mouth.'"

Frank picked up the two halves of the orb again. "Dare I look into the top compartment?" he asked.

"Do it," ordered the king. "I mean, if you wouldn't mind."

Frank lifted the lid and dozens of miniscule insects flew out.

"Those are the little devils!" shouted Fabian, pawing at them.

"Leave them, Your Majesty. They are perfectly harmless," said Cook.

"You sure?"

"Absolutely. Fairy flies. I love fairy flies!"

"Why would someone give me a present full of flies and ants?"

"Well, yes, that is the question, Your Majesty."

Frank was thinking. "The necklace was wrapped up, wasn't it?" he asked.

"That's right," said the king. "Very thoroughly. Took you a while to get all the paper off."

"They figured the little flies and ants would only escape once you put the necklace on," said Frank slowly. "They are absolutely tiny those flies. I've never seen them before."

"Yes," replied Cook. "You wouldn't have done. You don't get fairy flies in Gabsland any more than you get fire ants."

"Where do you find them?"

"Hipnia."

"Interesting. Nowhere else?"

"No, just there."

"And where do you find red fire ants?"

"Hipnia."

"Well, how strange," said Fabian. "This orb was a present from the Spams."

CHAPTER SIXTEEN

Ella squelched across the lawn. Simon and Spudbug came to see if she needed help.

"Are you all right?" Simon asked courteously.

"Course she is. Little dunk never hurt anyone, did it?" said Spudbug.

"I'm fine," said Ella. "Sorry about all that."

"How is your father?" asked Spudbug pointedly.

"Oh, you know him," laughed Ella. "He can be a little eccentric, but he always gets the

204

big calls right. It's what makes him such an incredible general."

Even she didn't believe that.

Spudbug came in close. "**Princess Ella, I will pay you the compliment of being honest with you. I admire the way you handle yourself –** given the example set by your parents."

"What's wrong with my parents?" said Ella. "Actually, don't answer that."

"I'm not trying to insult our hosts, don't get me wrong, but your father has been acting in a very peculiar manner all day and your mother has her ... eccentricities."

Ella was never slow in criticizing her parents, but she did not like anyone else doing so. She felt her hackles rising. "**She does not.**"

Simon gently touched her arm. "**Princess Ella, she is getting the Bishop of Gabsland to**

205

read her the last rites as we speak."

Ella looked over and, sure enough, the bishop was saying the prayers to her mother that are said to people who are about to die. Her mother, of course, was not about to die. She was just enjoying the idea that she might be. An unusual idea of fun to most people, but everyone finds joy in different places.

"My mother is a wonderful woman and a wonderful mother and a wonderful queen, and if you are going to be mean about her then I think that says more about you than it does about her," said Ella firmly. **"Shall we go to lunch?"**

"Ella," said Spudbug. **"I must be honest. You know, and I know, that today is not going well for your father. He flaked out for the inspection so that boy had to do it, sideways. And now the king's been twitching and flapping**

at nothing during the acrobatics. Not to mention the screaming and the scratching. If he can't handle hosting us for a day, how can we have confidence he can organize the repayment of our debt?" She sighed. "We know exactly how painful it will be for Gabsland to have to repay that money all in one go; we know what it would mean and accordingly we have resisted that course of action. But, seeing how chaotic your father is, this is the first time I've actually considered doing it. I can't see any other way."

"We don't want this either," added Simon quietly, "but what we want even less is an unstable and turbulent country on our borders."

"He isn't unstable," Ella began, fighting back hot, angry tears. "He's a genius. I promise the rest of this day is going to be an amazing success and show you what an incredible leader he is and how on top of everything he is. Now. Lunch. It's time for lunch. Shall we head back to the house? I think you'll love what Cook has prepared."

Simon and Spudbug looked at each and shook their heads.

As they walked back to the palace they passed the kitchen and through the open door they could see Fabian sitting in the bathtub, playing with a rubber duck and singing **"Incey Wincey Spider"**.

Ella changed out of her wet clothes, dried her hair and came down to the kitchen as soon as she could. There was no one there. Cook and Frank had left Fabian to bathe in peace and the king had finished washing, applied the cream and gone back upstairs feeling much better.

Ella had a look around. Frank had his own little place to work. A chopping board, a sink to do the washing up, a tub for vegetable peelings, some knives. His apron was folded neatly on his stool; a half-drunk glass of milk sat on the bench. It was so self-contained and simple. Ella felt a pang of jealousy. It seemed a nice life to her: dirty plates arrived, he washed them; vegetables needed peeling, he peeled them; onions needed chopping, he chopped them. He was given a task and he did the task.

That must be satisfying, she thought. She had no real purpose. She could and did wander the palace and the gardens, but talking to anyone but Dimmock and her maid, Daisy, was frowned upon. She was a princess and expected to hang out with her equals. Her only equals, though, were her parents. Ella was lonely and bored most of the time.

Frank bounded into the kitchen. Ella grinned at him. Frank was easy to be around. *He was one of those people*, she thought, *who make you feel like everything will probably work out for the best*. Unlike, say, her father, who always gave the impression that disaster was just around the corner.

Quickly, Frank filled her in on the necklace, the red fire ants and the fairy flies.

"That settles it," said Ella. "We need to talk to Dimmock. Too much strange stuff has been happening today and he's the only one who can help."

As they walked through the palace to the dungeons they discussed the day's odd events. Ella was relieved to hear that there was a rational explanation for her father's behaviour at the acrobatic display.

"It doesn't explain why he was being so weird at the inspection of the troops, though," she said thoughtfully. "It's almost like someone wants to make sure this Day of Celebration is ruined."

"The Hipneys," said Frank. "That's the only place which has those fairy flies and red fire ants."

He frowned. "But the necklace came from

Spamon. It doesn't
make any sense!"

At the dungeon entrance sat Small Dods,
the dungeon master. Neither Ella nor Frank
had ever met him before, but he was famous in
the palace. He never left his underground post.
The rumour was he hadn't seen sunlight for

fifteen years. His name was ironic; he was so tall he couldn't stand upright in the underground corridors that led to the cells without banging his head on the ceiling. Small Dods was as tall as Ella and Frank put together and as thin as a rake. He wore round spectacles, dungarees and had an entirely smooth and hairless head. He could be highly sarcastic.

"**Good morning,**" said Frank brightly.

"**I believe you mean good afternoon. It is after midday,**" said Small Dods.

"**Quite right,**" said Ella. "**Good afternoon. We would like to talk to Dimmock, please.**"

"**Sorry,**" said the stooped Small Dods. "**Orders of the king. No visitors.**"

"**I'm Princess Ella,**" said Princess Ella.

"**And I'm a bucket of lady frogs,**" said Small Dods.

"I'm sorry, what?" said Ella.

"If you're Princess Ella, then I'm a bucket of lady frogs."

"Right," said Ella. "But I really am Princess Ella."

"Oh sure," said Small Dods, "and I really am a bucket of lady frogs."

"She is Princess Ella," said Frank. "I promise you."

"Princess Ella would never come down to the dungeon," said Small Dods. "She's a princess. This is no place for royalty."

"I have a reason," said Ella. "I want to talk to Dimmock. He knows me. Ask him."

"Please," added Frank.

"Yes, please," said Ella.

Small Dods sighed.

"We really need to talk to Dimmock. This

214

is literally the most important thing ever," said Frank.

Small Dods sighed again. "You make me weary," he said. "Why did you have to use 'literally' incorrectly? Now I'm annoyed."

Ella and Frank just looked at him.

"Why do I bother?" said Small Dods. "Let's check your identity. Follow me."

The corridor to the cells was long and gloomy, snaking back and forth. Before they could see the cells they could hear Roger.

"And that's just the morning workout! Three sets of forty basic squats, two sets of thirty wall squats, eight sets of ten single-leg squats, eight sets of twelve side squats, eight sets of sixteen split squats, and, if I'm feeling up to it, some lateral curtsy squats..."

"Princess Ella!" said Dimmock as the

visitors rounded the last corner, sounding both surprised to see her and relieved to have a reason to stop Roger talking.

"**Literally!**" replied Ella. Small Dods turned to the princess and bowed low.

"**Apologies, Your Royal Highness,**" he said. "**I am embarrassed.**"

"No," said Ella. "**You are a box of lady frogs. Thank you for taking us to Dimmock. You may hop along.**"

Small Dods headed back to his post. Roger and Dimmock came over to the bars of the cell.

"**I am so sorry to see you in here, Dimmock,**" said Ella.

"**My lady!**" shouted Roger before Dimmock could reply. "**A fulsome welcome from we sorry wretches, unjustly detained at your father's pleasure. Banged up like a couple of kippers.**

We beg you to make entreaties to your father to secure our release. As I am fond of saying..."

"Roger, put a sock in it, there's a good chap," said Ella. "Why don't you go to the back of the cell and do some squats? Thank you so much."

Roger smiled a tight smile, bowed his head ever so slightly and did as he was told.

All these grown men, thought Frank, *obeying every command of this girl*. So odd. No one would ever do what he told them to do, but they jumped at Ella's every wish. She had power because of who her parents were and he had none because his parents were just ordinary people. At least, he assumed they were. His parents had died when he was a baby and he had been taken in by Cook.

They filled Dimmock in on the events of the

morning as quietly as they could so that Roger couldn't overhear.

"Well," said Dimmock at last, "what an extraordinary day. Let me see if I've got this right. The Spams gave a present, the orb full of insects, which seemed deliberately designed to agitate the king. They would have known how jumpy His Majesty is and how he'd be unable to cope with something like that with any degree of calm. That seems to point to the Spams being the culprits. And yet, those fairy flies and ants are only found in Hipnia."

"I know," said Ella. "Which doesn't make any sense!"

"And why bother?" asked Frank. They both turned to look at him and he flushed. "I mean, no offence, Ella, but the king didn't exactly need biting ants to behave ... unusually. We already knew that the Spams and the Hipneys might want their money back today."

"That's true," said Dimmock. "That was always a possibility. This Day of Celebration was a last-ditch effort. Why bother making King Fabian look more unstable than he already is?" He glanced at Ella. "No offence, my dear."

"None taken," said Ella absently. "So, someone wanted to be sure we had to repay the money now. But who?"

"The Hipneys always do things by committee," said Dimmock. "Perhaps Simon wanted to convince his people that it was the right thing to do."

"Do you think Simon did it then?" asked Ella.

"Maybe," said Dimmock. "Tell me, what present did the Hipneys give King Fabian?"

"Oh, just two cakes," said Ella. "Simon's mother baked them."

"Did anyone eat them?"

"The king ate one of them."

"Where's the other one?"

"In the kitchen," said Frank.

"Interesting," said Dimmock. "Can you get me that cake? I have a theory I want to test out."

"I'll go and get it now," said Frank and he ran to the kitchen.

Frank returned quickly with the other cake and handed it to Dimmock.

"Roger," said Dimmock. Roger paused mid bicep curl. "The queen sent you this. I think she's feeling guilty about putting you in here. Do you want it?"

Roger sauntered over.

"Ah, cake," he oozed. "Sugary treat of the gods. Come hither, little cupcake. I mean to eat you."

And he ate it.

"A bit stodgy," he said, popping the last crumb into his mouth. "But nice."

"Listen," said Dimmock when Roger had retreated to the back of the cell. "The grand luncheon is coming up. This is your chance to watch and observe. I have another suggestion to make."

"What?" asked Frank and Ella breathlessly.

"If my theory is right, then someone has planned to sabotage today and guarantee our failure. That means they are relying on us following the itinerary. I would suggest you change the plan for this afternoon and watch very carefully to see who seems most put out. If anyone has a plan then they won't like it if it is disrupted. Instead of releasing the peace balloons, why don't you suggest a horse ride?"

"All right," said Ella. "I don't think the king will even notice."

"I doubt it, Your Highness," said Dimmock. "I suggest that the king, Simon and Spudbug go riding together. Say it's to make up for the king not being at the inspection. See what happens. Come back after lunch and let's talk again."

CHAPTER SEVENTEEN

Simon and Googie were already waiting when Frank and Princess Ella got to the dining hall.

"Ah, good afternoon, princess. Are we early or is everyone else late?" said Simon. "It was 1 p.m. for lunch, wasn't it? Did we get that wrong or did someone else?"

Ella wanted to say what does it matter? The Hipneys were exhausting. "I'm starving!" she said, ignoring their question. "Don't know about you, but I could eat a horse." She knew

223

as soon as she said it that this was not the right thing to say to the Hipneys.

Simon stiffened and Googie shook her head.

"**We would never condemn you for your dietary choices,**" said Simon earnestly. "**We believe in the right of the individual to free choice.**"

"I didn't mean I would actually eat a horse," Ella said. "It's just an expression."

"Language has power," said Googie. "If I said I was so hungry I wanted to eat you, Ella, how would you feel?"

"I would cover myself in salt and pepper and lie down on a plate."

Googie blinked.

"**This conversation has taken a turn,**" said Simon cautiously.

Ella smiled and turned to Frank. "**Frank,**

could we please get some water?" She told herself she needed to remain calm and not get annoyed, but Simon and Googie irritated her. At least, she thought, the Spams got on with living without constant and tedious self-reflection.

The door flew open.

"Hello, you mimsy prats!" shouted Spudbug. She marched over to her place and plonked herself down.

Major Junction followed and, as he walked across the room, he tripped slightly on the rug.

"You doofus!" shouted Spudbug. "Enjoy your trip, Junction?! Did you all see that?"

Major Junction tried to smile, but Ella noticed that he was clenching his jaw.

"What's your favourite insect, Major? A Stumble Bee? Hahahahaha!"

"Ha ha," said the major stiffly. "Yes, how clumsy of me."

Simon, Googie and Ella looked at their plates.

"You fall over so much we should call you Tim Ber! Hahahahaha!"

On second thoughts, Ella pondered, a bit of self-reflection might do the Spams some good.

"Right, I'm starving. I'm so hungry I could eat a baby elephant," said Spudbug.

Ella looked to Simon and Googie who simply stared into the middle distance.

"The king and queen will be here in a moment and we will eat," said Ella. "I'm not sure if elephant is on the menu."

The king arrived, feeling and looking much better. The queen, on the other hand, had changed into a voluminous black sack.

*

Lunch passed without incident. Frank managed not to make any mistakes as butler, the king didn't say anything too weird, Simon and Googie enjoyed their lentils and Spudbug wasn't too rude. As Frank cleared away the dishes, Ella decided this was her moment.

"We've got a small change to the itinerary, I do hope that's all right," she said briskly, watching Spudbug and Simon closely. **"The king was distraught that he couldn't inspect the troops this morning..."**

"Yes, a great shame," said Fabian. **"Nothing**

like a good inspection."

"And we thought it might be a nice idea to get out into the countryside this afternoon."

"Meaning?" said Spudbug.

"We're all going riding. A good opportunity to talk and enjoy the beautiful Gabslandian countryside."

"Oooh," said Googie softly. "I think we need a vote on that, Simon."

"Is this wise, Supreme Leader?" said Major Junction. "You always say that Spams do not deviate from their plans."

"Nonsense! Bring it on! I bet I'm a better rider than either of them," said Spudbug.

"We'll see about that," said Simon. "All right. Horse riding it is."

CHAPTER EIGHTEEN

Small Dods pushed his glasses back up his nose.

"Follow me, Your Highness. And you, Frank. You'll need to see this."

As they snaked back along the winding corridor they could, again, hear Roger before they saw him. But this time he sounded different.

"You keep saying you're Dimmock and I'm Roger, but I really don't know any more," he was saying. "Maybe I'm Dimmock and you're Roger? My elbow can speak eight languages. I have a wolf called Jeremy in my armpits. Come out, Jeremy! Maybe I spangle Farouk divot kerplunk wibble ironing board arctic fox half a sixpence. Is that chicken called Lesley? My best friend is a tomato." Then he laid down and went to sleep.

Ella and Frank rushed to the bars of the cell where Dimmock was waiting for them.

"The cake!" said Dimmock triumphantly. "It had something in it that makes people behave in a very peculiar way. Look at him." They peered through the bars at Roger, who was dozing on his exercise mat. "Your father ate one, Ella. That's why he acted so strangely before the inspection of the troops."

"The Spam gift and the Hipney gift – both designed to make him look bad," said

Ella. "This afternoon should be interesting. We need to determine which country is so desperate."

"Could someone turn out the lights?" murmured Roger. "And bring me a cup of cocoa."

"We're no closer to finding out whether it's Spudbug or Simon sabotaging the day," Ella groaned. "And Major Junction and Googie are always at their side. We need to try and talk to the leaders alone, on this horse ride, and get them to reveal the truth."

"How will you do that?" asked Dimmock.

"Yes," said Ella. "That is the question."

*

It was time for the horse ride. Ella and Frank took King Fabian to the stables. Ella gave him a pep talk as they walked.

"You are such pleasant company, father, when you are relaxed. Just enjoy the ride. Talk to them about our beautiful scenery, the waterfalls, meadows and interesting trees."

"Will they want to talk about politics?" Fabian said anxiously. "You know I don't do politics."

"Well, if anyone tries to engage you in politics just say 'I think we should leave that for now and enjoy the beautiful outdoors.' Do you think you can do that?"

Fabian nodded. "If anyone tries to talk about politics, I say 'I think we should leave that for now and enjoy the beautiful outdoors, do you think you can do that?'"

"Good. But you don't have to say 'do you think you can do that?'"

"Got it," said Fabian. "If someone wants to talk about politics I say 'I think we should leave that for now and enjoy the beautiful outdoors, do you think you can do that, you don't have to say do you think you can do that.' Got it. Seems quite long, I hope I remember it all."

Ella took a deep breath. "New plan," she said. "If someone wants to talk about politics you say 'no politics!'"

"No politics!"

"That's it."

They were nearly at the stables. Ella could see that Simon was there and he had Googie with him. They seemed, Ella thought, to be having quite a heated discussion.

"I've told you," snapped Simon, as they approached. "I may not be any better than anyone else, but in this case I do know better!"

"Sorry," said Fabian in Ella's ear. "Do I say 'no politics, that's it' or just 'no politics'?"

"Just 'no politics.'"

"Got it. Simon!"

Simon and Googie turned to face them. Their expressions were irritable, but Ella noticed that Simon quickly plastered on a smile.

"Hello, Your Majesty. Looking forward to the ride?"

"NO POLITICS!" shouted Fabian in Simon's face.

"No problem!" said a startled Simon. "Your Majesty, would it be possible for Googie to join us? She is most keen."

"Yes!" said Fabian.

"No!" said Ella. This did not fit with her

plans to separate the leaders from their assistants. "I'm afraid we don't have a horse for Googie. Frank was going to give Googie and Major Junction a tour of the grounds. We have some of the finest topiaries you will ever see."

Googie flinched. "Those poor, tortured plants! I simply couldn't. Besides" – she smiled sweetly – "it's a dream of mine to ride with King Fabian."

"There's no horse."

Googie tilted her head to the side. "Perhaps you would let me ride *your* horse?"

"My horse ... oh, look, it's Supreme Leader Spudbug!"

Ella turned to greet the Spam leader, grateful to have a chance to stop talking to Googie and saw something that made her heart sink.

Spudbug was riding over on her huge horse and trotting along behind her was Major Junction on his pony, his feet touching the ground.

"Major," said Ella. "I hadn't realized you were planning on riding."

"The horses are rested," said the major gruffly. "Spam horses are made of strong stuff. You don't mind if I join, do you?"

"Oh, well, if you're riding your own horses that will free up a horse for me!" said Googie. "I get to come after all!"

Ella and Frank glanced at each other. There was nothing they could do at this point without giving the game away.

"Excellent!" said Ella. "Well, we have quite a group now. You should come too, Frank. Can't leave you behind if everyone's going."

Frank tried to smile, but getting back on

a horse was the last thing he wanted to do. **"Thank you, Your Royal Highness. I'll go and saddle up."**

Frank walked into the stable with a heavy heart. He looked at Cheeseballs and Cheeseballs looked at him. Frank felt as if they were both thinking the same thing – *not again*. Frank placed the ladder against the horse and climbed up into the saddle.

"Hello, Cheeseballs, my old friend," Frank said. **"Now, this time, I'm in charge. You hear me? I'm the boss."**

He gave the horse a nudge with his heels but nothing happened. He tried again a little harder. Still nothing. Ella walked in.

"We have to find a way to separate Simon and Spudbug," she hissed. "And find out which of them is behind this."

"Right," said Frank. "And then?"

"No idea, but we'll never get them to confess with everyone watching." Ella raised her hand to slap Cheeseballs on the backside.

"Wait!" said Frank. "Don't slap him. Remember what happened last time."

"Oh, yes," said Ella. She grinned and slapped the horse anyway.

Cheeseballs reared up, Frank clutched at its neck, and the horse bolted out of the stable. This time, though, Frank didn't panic. He took the reins and pulled gently, bringing Cheeseballs to a smooth stop next to Spudbug and her horse.

"Hi," said Frank.

"Hey, kid." Spudbug looked around to see if they could be overheard. She leaned over to him and said quietly, **"You know who's been talking to me about you?"**

Frank froze. Did she know he suspected her of sabotage?

The colour drained from Frank's face and he could feel his body starting to shake. He wasn't cut out for all this high-level intrigue and drama. He was a kitchen boy. He peeled potatoes and carrots. He washed dishes. Was Spudbug going to tear him to pieces with her bare hands? Who would stop her?

She leaned in closer. **"I said: do you know who's been talking to me about you?"**

Frank couldn't speak. His mouth was as dry as sawdust. He couldn't swallow. He shook his head.

"Nobody," said Spudbug. **"Nobody was talking about you."**

Frank stared at her, not understanding.

Spudbug threw her head back and roared with laughter. **"It's a joke! Nobody was talking about you because you're a nobody! Get it?"**

"Oh." Frank managed a small smile. **"Ha ha."**

Spudbug thumped him good-naturedly on the back and nearly knocked him off his horse. **"Top banter, right there,"** she said. **"Now then,** everyone here? Shall we go? Try and keep up, slow-coaches."

The others joined them: Googie was stroking her horse's mane; Ella frowning in thought; Frank still shaking; Major Junction put his feet in the stirrups, which meant his knees were up near his ears.

Simon said, **"Happy to do what the group wants to do, after proper consultation."**

And Fabian shouted, **"No politics!"**

"Great," said Spudbug. **"Let's ride."**

CHAPTER NINETEEN

The horses walked through the topiary garden with the weird and wonderful plant shapes. This was Ella's favourite part of the grounds. She used to play alone here for hours when she was small, pretending that the animal shapes were her friends. Later today they were going to unveil a new plant sculpture in honour of the state visit. It was to be the climax of the day and the moment Fabian – and all of Gabsland – hoped that the Spams and the Hipneys would agree to give the Gabslandians more time to repay their debts.

The new bush statue was hidden under a huge sheet, ready for the grand reveal later. As they walked past it, the group chatted amiably in the afternoon sunshine. It was a lovely day and sitting on horseback, riding through the beautiful gardens, it was easy to think that all was right with the world. Ella and Frank had to remind themselves that one or more people within this group were trying to sabotage any hope of peace and bring about the downfall of Gabsland.

Ella chatted to Spudbug, but her mind was elsewhere. How to split up the group? And even if they managed that, then what? How could two children stop ruthless and single-minded, clever, political operators?

How she longed for Dimmock to be here. This was the kind of crisis he had made short work of so many times in the past. The rest of the country thought Fabian was the hero, but Ella had spotted what was going on long ago. But, of course, Dimmock wasn't there. He wasn't there because, the rumour was, he had farted. Was one little fart really going to plunge them all into total chaos? Ella hated to admit it, but right now that looked the most likely outcome.

Spudbug was droning on about herself, about how good she was at everything and how bad Major Junction was at everything. Spudbug's self-esteem seemed to require not just her to succeed but Major Junction to fail. Major Junction listened to it all with a rictus, and occasionally said things like "haha yes, I'm useless" and "that's why you're the Supreme Leader and not me".

That gave Ella an idea.

By now they had walked through the grounds of the palace, past the old oak tree with the hollowed-out trunk, beyond the yew hedge and through the great gates into the woods beyond. Ella trotted forward to join Frank and quickly whispered, **"I'm going to suggest something to everyone and when I do you need to hang back with Major Junction."** She then wheeled around and shouted to Spudbug, **"I bet I'm a better jumper than you!"**

Spudbug gave a roar of laughter. **"Now, that's fighting talk, young lady! I hope you know what you're letting yourself in for."**

Ella pointed at the fields ahead. **"Three**

fields, a hedge between each one. Each hedge bigger than the one before. Think you've got what it takes?"

"Don't get cocky, Princess."

"I'm warning you, the last jump is not easy."

"Bring it on."

"What about you, Simon?"

"I don't want to get into a competition," said Simon. "Creating winners creates losers too—"

"Oh bore off!" shouted Spudbug, spurring her horse on. "Last one over all the hedges is a big frilly blouse!"

Spudbug raced off with Ella in hot pursuit. Simon and Googie looked at each other.

"Competition isn't the Hipney way unless it's agreed by a proper vote," said Simon.

"Besides, I wouldn't want you to feel bad."

"What do you mean?" said Googie. "Why would I feel bad?"

"Well ... I'd probably ... there's a good chance I'd..."

"I'm a better jumper than you."

"With respect—"

"I SO AM!!"

"FINE, COME ON THEN!"

Simon and Googie encouraged their horses into action and galloped towards the first hedge.

Fabian said, "What's happening?"

"A race, Your Majesty," said Frank.

"Ooh, yippee!" shouted Fabian, riding off after the others.

That left Major Junction and Frank. Frank looked at the major half-sitting, half-standing on his tiny horse and realized what Ella was up to. That horse could never jump those hedges.

"There's a path around the fields. Shall we take that?" Frank said.

"I suppose," said Major Junction sniffily. "I could jump those hedges on Monster here, but I don't feel like it."

"Monster?" said Frank. "Interesting name." The horse couldn't look more placid and less like a monster, but then looks could be deceiving.

"Yes, let's take the path and let's hurry up about it," snapped Major Junction.

They turned and took the path that followed the perimeter of the field. It was a much further trip than the dash across the middle of the field. Major Junction, who seemed irritated to be separated from the others, urged Monster to get a move on, but the tiny horse was struggling under the major's weight.

Frank was sitting way above him on his much larger horse so conversation was difficult. Frank tried anyway. After all, maybe he could glean some information about Spudbug from her second in command. Perhaps the major knew if she was up to something and might let it slip? *I must be subtle*, thought Frank.

"Are you enjoying your trip?"

There was no reply from Major Junction. Frank tried again.

"Very pretty here, isn't it? Is Spam countryside similar?"

Frank looked down at Major Junction who looked very red in the face. Frank realized

249

that Junction was helping Monster to move more quickly by lifting his bodyweight off him and running with his legs still straddling the horse. It looked awkward and uncomfortable.

"So, between us," said Frank confidentially, "what are the chances of you Spams wanting your money back now after today? Has the king, er, impressed Spudbug with his calm in the face of adversity?"

The major snorted. "If anything, today has made things worse for you Gabslandians."

"Why?" said Frank eagerly.

"Spudbug didn't want to do anything," the major said, trotting along and sweating heavily. "Spudbug is all talk and no action! But now she's seen how incredibly incompetent your so-called king is, she's come around to the idea that your time is up. And maybe that's not such a bad thing. Are we nearly there? Come on, Monster, step on it."

CHAPTER TWENTY

Ella was an expert rider. It was one of the few things she looked forward to doing every day and she often went out on her horse for hours at a time. She and Spudbug both cleared the first hedge with no trouble. Spudbug had a head start, but Ella was gaining on her with every stride.

"I'm coming for you, Supreme Leader!" shouted Ella.

"No chance, girlie!" Spudbug yelled back.

They reached the next fence at the same time and both horses took off, gliding gracefully through the air side by side, high over the wide hedge and landed with a thud on the other side.

Spudbug whooped and urged her horse on.

"Now *this* is fun!" she shouted.

"You won't enjoy it when I beat you!" countered Ella, laughing.

Behind them Simon and Googie were neck and neck too. This race had unleashed something deep within them, but there was no joy in it, just a desperate desire to beat each other. They were level as they raced across the second field; neither looked across at the other but maintained total focus on the task in hand. Googie's jaw was clenched tight; Simon wasn't blinking. They hit the second jump and Simon's horse landed first. He was ahead, just.

He let out a primal roar. Googie tightened her grip on the reins and urged her horse on.

Some distance back, King Fabian was taking it easy. He enjoyed riding but was not hugely fond of going too fast. He chatted away amiably to his horse.

"Oh, look, Parsnip, there's a daisy. I like

daisies. Nice flower. How long has it been since I made a daisy chain? Probably fifteen years. I should make a daisy chain. That would be nice. In fact, let's stop here and make one now."

Fabian jumped down and started collecting daisies.

Up ahead, Ella and Spudbug approached the final hedge side by side. This last hurdle was big, but Ella knew it was perfectly possible to jump. She had done so many times. Nothing separated the two riders and their horses were well matched. In the final few strides before the jump, Ella made her move. She stood up in the stirrups and, as her horse leapt into the air, threw herself, deliberately, off her horse and into a haystack on the far side of the hedge, hitting it with some force. The horse landed then slowed up and stopped, confused as to what had happened to its rider.

Spudbug had landed on the far side of the fence first and took off round the field doing a lap of honour screaming **"Champioooooooooooonnnnnnnnnnnnnnnn!"** and punching the air in delight.

Behind them, Simon had seen Ella's tumble.

"Princess Ella has fallen," he called to Googie. **"We should stop and check on her."**

"Nice try, Simon," shouted Googie. Her eyes were wild, her jaw set. **"*You* can stop if you want. I'm going to beat you over that hedge."**

"She might have hurt herself."

"Do you think I was born yesterday? Prepare to lose, loser!"

At the hedge they jumped together and landed together.

"I won!" shouted Googie.

"Rubbish!" yelled Simon.

They jumped off their horses and faced each other.

"Rubbish?" cried Googie. "That's all you think of me, isn't it? You don't listen to me and you don't ever let me have my say. Well, this time *I* won, OK?"

Simon put his hands up. "Googie, please. This is neither the time nor the place."

"Oh, should we hold a committee meeting?" screamed Googie. "A focus group? You're a spineless, weak, hopeless leader and you make me want to hurl!!!"

Breathing hard, shaking her head furiously, Googie stomped off across the field away from him.

That, thought Ella, *is a huge over-reaction.*

"Are you all right?" Simon shouted to Ella as he ran over.

"I think I hurt my ankle," said Ella, "but it's not too bad."

Spudbug rode back from her lap of honour still whooping. As she passed Googie going the other way she taunted her, "You only sing when you're winning! Sing when you're wiiiinnnnnnnnniiiiiiinnnnnnngggggggg!"

"Shove it," said Googie moodily.

"Hahahahahaha!" laughed Spudbug. She rode up to Ella and Simon kneeling beside her. "What happened to you?"

"Fell off," said Ella.

Spudbug looked at her for a few seconds. "You still lost," she said. "Loser. I'm going back. Where's Major Disappointment?"

"Must be with the butler boy," said Simon.

"Listen, Ella," said Spudbug, "Simon and I have something to tell you."

Ella sat up. "What is it?"

Spudbug looked back into the next field where the king was making his daisy chain and talking to his horse.

"We didn't want to demand the money back today," she said. "We just wanted to wind your father up a bit. We thought today would get us some nice trade deals and a few good meals but we never really wanted to dismantle your country. Did we, Simon?"

Simon shook his head. "That isn't good for anyone, but, then – well – your father couldn't get it together to inspect the troops. He lost it during the acrobatics display. He can't even manage a horse ride. He's not a ruler, Ella. I'm sorry, but he's not. He's all over the place. Where has all the money gone?"

"Are you saying you're going to demand

we repay immediately?" said Ella miserably. "Both of you?"

Simon and Spudbug nodded.

"I don't think we have a choice," said Simon kindly.

"I hate to say it," said Spudbug, "but he's right."

A field away, King Fabian placed a large daisy chain around his horse's neck.

"You're such a good boy, yes you are!" he said to the animal affectionately. "And so am I."

CHAPTER TWENTY-ONE

Frank and Major Junction said not a word to each other all the way back. Once they reached the palace, the major headed off to brush down Monster. Frank went down to the kitchen.

"There you are!" said Cook. "Princess Ella was looking for you and I need help with the carrots."

"There's a lot going on, Cook. Can you do the carrots this time?"

"Absolutely not! As my old uncle used to

261

say, 'A carrot in time saves nine.' I have dinner to prepare for our very important guests. You are the kitchen boy, get on with it."

"But ... there's ... we think..." Frank gave up. He could hardly tell Cook that he and Ella suspected someone was sabotaging the Day of Celebration in the hope of bringing Gabsland to its knees.

"Fine," he said, and began peeling.

Ella came in. Cook became flustered.

"Oh, Your Majesty! Twice in one day! Well, this is special. Would you like a crumpet?"

"No, thank you."

"A piece of cake?"

"Not for me, thank you."

"Flapjack?"

"I'm not hungry. Thank you all the same. I need to speak to Frank." Ella crossed the kitchen to Frank. **"What are you doing?"** she asked him.

"Peeling carrots."

"Can I do some?"

"What?! Yes, I suppose."

"Great!" she said. **"Show me how."**

"You don't know how to peel a carrot?"

"Why would I?"

"Good point."

They stood side by side over the bowl.

"We have to expose the plot and quickly," said Ella to Frank, as quietly as she could so that Cook wouldn't hear. "They have decided my father is unable to handle things properly. If we make accusations without proof now, they will say we are clutching at straws to hang on to our kingdom. It would be easy to dismiss us as desperate. We need proof and we need it now."

"But we haven't got any!"

"You must remain calm. We must both remain calm." Ella took a couple of deep breaths. She was shaking as she peeled her carrot. "What did you find out on the ride back?"

"Only that Major Junction is possibly the moodiest man I have ever met. He did *not* enjoy our detour one bit. Wouldn't say a word to me the whole time." He thought for a moment. "Actually, he did say one thing. He said that Spudbug didn't want to make us pay back the money when she got here, but that she'd changed her mind. He sounded pleased about that."

"I see," said Ella thoughtfully. "Well, I learnt that Googie is one stressed-out woman with some serious underlying anger issues."

They were silent for a while as they peeled their vegetables. "Interesting, isn't it? Neither Spudbug or Simon wanted us to pay our debt immediately, until everything went wrong today."

"I wonder..." said Frank.

"What?"

"I wonder if we've been thinking about this all wrong." He put down the carrot he was peeling. "We've both assumed it must be either Spudbug or Simon out to sabotage the Day of Celebration. But what if it was someone else? Or ... *two* other people. Two people who hate each other, but who have actually been working together."

"You mean..."

"That's right," said Frank. "I reckon Major Junction and Googie have been the saboteurs all along. We need a plan."

"I have an idea," said Ella. "Pass me another carrot and I'll tell you it."

*

In the dungeon, Roger had woken up and begun talking again.

"Listen, wall," he was saying to the wall, "I

have been told that walls have ears. Where are your ears? Where are they?"

Dimmock sighed. He wondered how Frank and Ella were getting on. He wondered when he'd get out of here. And he wondered how much trouble the kingdom of Gabsland was in.

*

In the royal bedroom, the king and queen were preparing for the unveiling of the topiary statue. The king was changing his clothes. The queen was already dressed in her favourite gown: a full-length jet-black silk dress with a long train. She lay on the bed with her arms across her chest and her eyes closed.

"**Do you know I had forgotten how beautiful our country is?**" the king was saying.

"It's stunning. I sat for a long time in a field and I made a daisy chain and I thought about you. I wished you could have been there." He looked out of the windows at the gardens. "I'm very lucky, that's what I thought. Very lucky to be king of this great land and very lucky to have you."

Though she had heard everything, the queen said nothing. For a moment, she felt her heart rate quicken, she felt more ... alive. She'd forgotten what that felt like, but she enjoyed it.

CHAPTER TWENTY-TWO

Major Junction was meticulous in the way he cared for Monster. Major Junction was meticulous about everything. His trousers had the sharpest crease of any in the army, his shoes were perfectly polished and his moustache always immaculately trimmed, combed and oiled.

He had cleaned Monster's hooves, dislodged dirt from his coat with a curry comb, then given him a good going over with a body brush, combed his mane and tail – taking care to detangle any matted hair – and then plaited them. Only when Monster looked the way the major wanted him to look did he leave the stable and head back to the palace to get changed for the unveiling.

Major Junction was not in a good mood. He had not enjoyed being separated from the main group earlier. He had not enjoyed being made to feel inferior to the others because his horse couldn't jump. He had not enjoyed the ignominy of having to ride with the butler. Or, even worse, the butler's stand-in's stand-in! Major Tony Junction had hated being made to sit at the kids' table when he was a boy at big family occasions. Junction had always felt like a grown-up, even as a child, and now he finally *was* a grown-up and today he'd missed out on riding with the grown-ups and had been condemned to the kids' riding group.

He walked as though marching: rigid arms swinging back and forth, stiff bearing. He passed Princess Ella.

"Good evening, Major," she said.

"Good evening, Your Royal Highness," he replied, as stiffly as he walked. He continued towards the palace.

"Did she find you?" came the princess's voice from behind him.

He stopped and turned. **"I beg your pardon?**

Did who find me?"

"I'm sure it wasn't important. Googie was looking for you; she seemed quite stressed, but she'll find you at the unveiling in half an hour, so don't worry. See you later!" The princess moved off.

"**Wait!**" said Major Junction. "I mean, I'm sure it's not important but ... where is she? In case it's important. Which it won't be."

"Now, let me think," said Ella, "she said she had to speak to someone else as well ... oh, who was it?"

"Sure you can't remember?" asked Major Junction with a tight chuckle.

"Oh, yes! I remember. She was looking for the bishop."

"The bishop?"

"Yes, that's right. She said she wanted to

speak to the bishop. She was quite upset. Hope she's all right. They're very sensitive, the Hipneys. See you later." Again, Ella turned to leave.

"Where might I find the bishop?" called Junction.

"Oh, he'll be down with Small Dods. He's ... I could show you? We have a little time before the unveiling."

"That would be most kind, Your Royal Highness."

Major Junction indicated that Princess Ella should take the lead, and they walked briskly towards the stairs that led down to the dungeon. Ella could feel her heart thumping in her chest. She was starting to have second thoughts. This was a dangerous plan, but it was the only one she could see having any chance of working.

"**After you,**" said the major as they reached the top of the stairs.

"**Thank you,**" said Ella as calmly as she could. She was aware her voice was shaking slightly. She could hear the major's boots on the stairs behind her. She didn't remember the journey down taking as long before.

They reached Small Dods's desk and Ella was relieved to see he wasn't there. So far, so good. Navigating the long corridors to the cells, Ella was also relieved that she couldn't hear Roger. Hopefully the effects of the cake had worn off by now.

As they rounded the last corner, she saw Roger in his cell sleeping, snoring heavily. Dimmock, sat next him, looked up as they came in. His face gave nothing away. In the

next cell sat Small Dods, the cell door open. Dods sat at a table, two empty chairs on the other side of it. There were full three cups of tea and a plate of biscuits on the table.

"Ah, **Small Dods**," said Ella. "**We were hoping to find the bishop and Googie.**"

"**Oh, they've just popped out,**" said Small Dods and laughed. He threw an arm over the back of his chair.

What is he doing? thought Ella. *He's trying to act casually but he can't act!*

"**Popped out in the** sense **of leaving a place for a short amount of time,**" Small Dods continued, "**not in the sense of leaping out from a place or in the sense of applying pressure to something to dislodge it.**" He tried to chuckle casually, but it came out more like the bark of a small dog.

"Do you know when they'll be back?" asked Ella, trying to get the conversation back on track.

"Any minute now," said Small Dods, ostentatiously looking at his watch. "And by that I do mean any minute. Could be within the next minute, the minute after that or possibly the minute after that. They have tea waiting."

"Well, we don't want to be late for the statue unveiling," said Ella. "Please could you run and find Googie and tell her we are waiting here for her."

"Certainly," said Small Dods, standing up to leave. "Now I will pop out and by that I mean—"

"Don't worry," said Major Junction. "I'll go look for her."

This was not in the plan.

Ella laughed. **"Oh, Major, you have no idea how confusing this palace is! You will get lost and we will never find you again! Small Dods, hurry up, please. Major, take a seat."**

Before the major could object or Small Dods could start talking again, Ella ushered Small Dods up and out.

"Biscuit?" offered Ella.

"No, thanks. I don't have all day," said the major.

He's not the most charming of men, Ella thought.

The major stood by the open door of the cell. This was not where Ella needed him to be. She had already offered him a seat. How to get him to move into the cell without being too obvious?

"**Oh!**" she said, staggering slightly. "**Oh!**"

"**Are you all right?**" said the major gruffly.

"**I'm fine,**" she said. "**I feel a little faint. Long day.**" She rested her hands on the table.

"**Would you mind bringing that chair over for me to sit down in?**" she said. "**I'm sorry to ask.**"

Major Junction did not hesitate. He ran over and placed a chair behind Ella. She knew he would have been brought up to be chivalrous, to hold doors open for women, to stand up when they entered a room and so on.

"**Can I get you something?**" he asked her.

"**Maybe one of those biscuits,**" she said.

As he offered her the plate, the sound of footsteps running down the corridor – Small Dods and Frank.

"I have a message from the king," said Frank, as they appeared. "We are instructed to detain Major Junction here in the cells."

"What are you talking about?" said Ella, leaping up and moving quickly to the cell door. "I won't hear of it! Major Junction is our guest!"

She was outside the cell in an instant and Major Junction rushed to follow her. But Small Dods was already in position and he slammed the cell door and locked it in one practised movement.

"Hey!" yelled the major.

"What are you doing?!" shouted Ella, sounding shocked and surprised. "Let him go *at once!* And that's an order."

"I'm sorry, Your Royal Highness," said Frank. "It seems Googie has confessed to the bishop that she and Major Junction were trying to disrupt the Day of Celebration so that Gabsland would be ruined."

"What are you talking about?! This is ridiculous!" said Ella. "I don't believe it for one second. Let him out!"

"Let me out this instant!" said Major Junction.

"Supreme Leader Spudbug has been informed and has consented to Major Junction being imprisoned until he can be questioned by the authorities."

"Listen to me," said Ella indignantly, "this is absolute nonsense! Googie may have been involved in some sort of plot – I don't entirely trust those Hipneys – but I refuse to believe a man of Major Junction's honesty and integrity would get mixed up in something like that! Let him out!"

"Orders from the king and Supreme Leader Spudbug. Sorry, Your Royal Highness."

Frank turned and left. Small Dods followed him.

Major Junction looked incandescent with rage. Ella ran to the bars of the cell.

"I will sort this out," she said to him. **"This is absurd."**

Major Junction could only nod curtly as Ella left. The major, so dumbfounded by what had just happened, stood in the cell with his mouth open. After a few seconds, he looked to the occupants of the other cell and caught Dimmock's eye. The butler shrugged.

The major scowled.

Dimmock said, "Perhaps, if I could give you one piece of advice, Major, it would be 'don't wake Roger.'"

CHAPTER TWENTY-THREE

Ella joined Small Dods and Frank at the entrance to the dungeons.

"I think I'm going to be sick," she said. "That was so difficult!"

"You did a great job," said Frank. "Seriously, I don't think I could have done that. I completely believed you were shocked and angry."

Ella puffed out her cheeks.

"So I guess we're really doing this!" she said.

They shared a nervous laugh.

"Right," she continued, "part one accomplished. Thank you, Small Dods."

"I thought I was pretty convincing," he said proudly.

Ella wanted to say, *Yeah, about as convincing as a rhinoceros wearing a wig and glasses to try and get into a humans-only restaurant*, but she just nodded. "This is perhaps the most important day in our country's history, Dods. If Roger recovers, why don't you take him and Dimmock to the unveiling later? I'll square it with the king. Might be good to have some support."

"Phase two," said Frank. "We need to hurry. Make sure he doesn't get out, Dods."

Leaving Small Dods to his underground domain, Frank and Princess Ella climbed back up the stairs to the main part of the palace. As they ran across the central hallway, the library door flew open and Supreme Leader Spudbug came charging out.

"Have you seen Major Junction?" she barked. She looked angry.

"No," lied Ella.

"Did he come back from the ride? He's probably sulking somewhere."

"We rode back together," said Frank. "I think he went to deal with his horse."

"Then I shall look there. And then can we get on with this unveiling? We will need to pack up and leave. The rest of our delegation are ready."

"Everything is ready in the gardens," said Ella. "I'll get the king and queen and, once you find Major Junction, we can begin. We have no wish to hold you up."

"Yes, let's not make this more difficult than it needs to be," said Spudbug, stomping off.

Ella and Frank looked at each other.

"It's all good," said Frank.

"Not sure 'all good' is the right phrase but, yeah, onwards," Ella replied. "To the next part of the plan. Just want to check on my parents first. You carry on with phase two – good luck."

They raced up the stairs. Frank dashed off down the corridor while Ella knocked on the door of the royal bedroom and went in without waiting for an answer. The queen was lying in her usual position on the bed, and the king was tying his tie.

"Time to do this," Ella said to her father. He took her hands in his.

"I have a good feeling that all will be well,"

said Fabian. "The day has gone smashingly. We're not going to have to pay back the money, I know it."

"Ye-es," said Ella. She couldn't tell him that Spudbug had said that they had already reached their decision and that they didn't think Fabian was up to leading Gabsland out of this mess. She needed him in a good frame of mind so that he wouldn't freak out and do something daft. But Ella felt scared and alone, knowing that her country was in so much trouble, and not being able to share it with her people.

"See you in the garden," she said. A sudden feeling of panic surged through her. "I love you both. You know that, yeah?"

This was not how Ella usually spoke to her family, and the queen, lying on the bed, was so shocked she opened her eyes and sat up.

"Is everything all right?" she asked Ella.

"Yes, darling, are you quite well?" asked Fabian.

"Yes!" said Ella. "Just felt affectionate. Sorry."

*

Frank had wasted no time. He knocked on Googie's door. She opened it.

"Yes?" she said.

"Cook has something she needs to discuss with you," Frank said.

"Cook?" said Googie, sounding bewildered. "It'll have to wait, I'm afraid. I have things to do."

"But," said Frank, "she says it's very important. She said it's a matter of life or death."

"Life or death?" snapped Googie, beginning to shut the door. "Seriously? Go bother someone else."

Frank shrugged. "I told Cook you wouldn't be interested. I told her to discuss it with Supreme Leader Spudbug. Right. Bye."

Googie hesitated. "She was going to talk to Spudbug?"

"Unless you can come and help." Frank looked at her hopefully.

"All right," Googie said at last. "I'll come down to the kitchen, but I can only give her two minutes."

"Thank you!" said Frank. "It'll get her off my back."

"After you," said Googie.

*

Ella ran down to the dungeons. Three members of the acrobat troupe were waiting for her. They were dressed in army outfits that didn't quite fit them.

"Thank you for doing this. All will become clear, but it is for the greater good of Gabsland," she said. "Come with me. Do you have the hood and rope?"

"We do."

"Let's go."

They followed the princess down the corridor and Small Dods joined them. No one spoke. Major Junction was standing by the door of his cell as they came in.

"Thank you, princess," he said. "I knew you wouldn't let them get away with this."

"Major Junction," said Ella sternly. "I have now spoken to Googie and to the bishop. I have also spoken to the king and to Supreme Leader Spudbug. There is no doubt in my mind that you are guilty."

He began to splutter. "What are you talking about?! This is outrageous!"

"I'll tell you what is outrageous, Major," said Ella hotly. "Drugging my father is outrageous. Filling an orb with red fire ants is outrageous. Attempting to undermine our king and the

292

whole country of Gabsland is outrageous."

Major Junction flushed red and looked at the floor.

"Your plan has been discovered, Major. We know everything; Googie has confessed to it all. You were plotting together to undermine the Day of Celebration, force us to repay the debt and bring the kingdom of Gabsland to its knees. The game is up. You will face the full force of the law. I am disgusted and disappointed. Soldiers will take you out of here right now and you will be transported to prison. Googie is already on her way there." She turned to the acrobats. "Take him away."

Ella swept out. Once she was around the corner and out of sight, she bent over with her hands on her knees and took a few deep breaths.

Behind her she heard the cell door being

opened and the acrobats grabbing the major. It sounded like he was putting up quite a fight. They bound his hands behind his back, tied the hood over his head and marched him out.

Ella stood and ran on ahead towards the kitchen.

CHAPTER TWENTY-FOUR

Frank led Googie into the kitchen. Cook was waiting.

"I'm here," Googie said. "What is it you need from me? And, with the greatest of respect, would you mind getting a bit of a move on? We've got this statue unveiling in a minute."

"Thank you for coming down," said Cook. "I don't know where to begin."

"May I suggest at the beginning?"

"From the beginning. Right. Some days I

make food and half of it isn't eaten."

"What a terrible shame," said Googie. "How can I help? How can I help quickly?"

"Last week I cooked a chicken pie with rice and they barely touched it! And everyone knows you can't reheat rice so I had to throw it all away!"

"Well, don't eat chicken – that would be my advice," said Googie. "Lentils can be reheated. But what's that got to do with...?"

"And don't even get me started on my lasagne," said Cook. "I make the best lasagne you'll ever taste. My old uncle used to say it was 'lasagne straight from the horse's mouth'. Did they eat it all? Did they, my foot?!"

"Lasagne?" Googie frowned. "Frank mentioned something about life and death?"

"Yes, indeed," said Cook. "It's my *life*

296

cooking for them and if they don't eat it, it'll be the *death* of me."

"Look, I need to go," said Googie. "Not that it hasn't been fascinating, but—"

"STOP!" Ella burst through the door with the other three acrobats, also dressed as soldiers. "There you are! We've searched the palace from top to bottom looking for you. Googie, you are under arrest."

"I'm what?"

"Grab her!" said Ella, and the acrobats jumped forward to seize Googie. "Major Junction has confessed to a plot to sabotage the Day of Celebration and he says that you were involved."

"A plot?" Googie shrieked and clasped a hand to her mouth. "What are you talking about?"

"He has told us everything. The necklace,

297

the cake – take her away."

"I don't know anything about this!" wailed Googie.

Frank decided Ella needed help. "Oh, yes," he said, "Major Junction told me everything during our ride together. I told him to confess to the bishop and he did."

Googie shook her head, looking utterly bewildered. *Either she was an excellent actress*, Ella thought uneasily, *or she really was innocent.* "Ella, please," Googie said softly. "I'm innocent."

Ella bit her lip. What if she had got this wrong? Major Junction, the second in command of the entire Spam nation, was tied up with a hood over his head in the back of a wagon, heading out of the palace grounds as they spoke! And now here she was attempting to imprison the second in command of the entire Hipney nation! If she was wrong, then the Spams and the Hipneys would show no mercy. The kingdom of Gabsland wouldn't survive.

Still, there was no going back now. They were in too deep.

"Take her away," she said to the acrobats. **"Into the wagon."**

Googie had tears in her eyes. **"What have you done, Ella? What have you done?"**

The acrobats placed a black hood over her head and tied it tight. They tied her arms behind her back and pushed her out of the door. Frank, Ella and Cook looked at each other; no one spoke for a few seconds, but they were all thinking the same thing. They were all imagining what might happen if they'd got this wrong. Horribly, irreversibly wrong.

"Phase three, let's go," said Ella and left the room.

CHAPTER TWENTY-FIVE

Major Junction was shoved into the acrobats' first wagon and tied to the bench seat. He had not stopped threatening the acrobats from the moment they had grabbed him in the dungeon.

"Supreme Leader Spudbug won't stand for this," he said to them. "When she hears about this she will tear you limb from limb."

The acrobats said not a word. They pushed the wagon through the palace gardens as quickly as they could, through the big metal gates and out into the countryside beyond.

Up in her room, Spudbug saw them leave. She narrowed her eyes. *These Gabslandians,* she thought, *are utterly hopeless. Why have three people push a wagon? Why not get a horse to pull it? Much more efficient.*

By the time the second wagon trundled up the drive and out of the palace gates, pushed by the remaining acrobats, Spudbug was heading down the palace staircase to the unveiling. Inside that wagon, Googie sat silently, tied to the bench, a black cloth hood over her head.

*

The pond in the palace topiary garden had at its centre a stone statue of King Fabian designed by famous Gabslandian artist, Julian Hindgut.

Hindgut was a master stoneworker who could be wildly temperamental. He was known to go into rages that lasted days, if not weeks.

For his thirtieth birthday, Queen Charlotte had gifted Fabian a statue to be created by the great Hindgut and a meeting was arranged to discuss the design. King Fabian told him that the artwork would be situated in the centre of their garden pond and Fabian wanted it to double up as a fountain.

"A fountain?" the great artist had said disdainfully. "You want water spraying out of you?"

"Well, yes," the nervous king had replied. "Yes, please."

Hindgut resented having his artistic vision dictated to like this, and that's how there came to be, in the middle of the royal pond in the gardens of the Gabslandian palace, a life-size stone statue of King Fabian III with water shooting from his open mouth, water spraying out of both his nostrils and water squirting from both his ears. What Fabian only realized some time later was that Julian Hindgut also made water dribble out of the bottom of the statue's left trouser leg so that it looked like the king was peeing his pants. The king and Julian Hindgut had not spoken since.

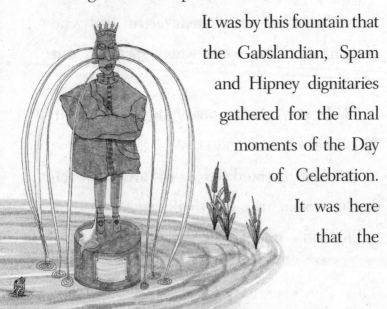

It was by this fountain that the Gabslandian, Spam and Hipney dignitaries gathered for the final moments of the Day of Celebration. It was here that the

Gabslandians had hoped all three countries would come to an arrangement that would allow Gabsland to survive. The topiary statue that was to be unveiled was close by, covered in a huge piece of cloth. King Fabian and Queen Charlotte, looking relaxed and happy for a change, were chatting to the bishop, who was surprised to see them holding hands. Supreme Leader Spudbug, looking tense and angry, was in a huddle with the other Spams, whispering intensely. Simon and the Hipneys looked tired and worried.

Ella and Frank watched them gather from a window in the palace.

"This is your big moment," she said to Frank. **"Will you be all right?"**

Frank said nothing. He tried to smile at her, but his nervousness was obvious.

"Let's go," she said.

The first wagon reached the stone bridge by the hollow oak. Major Junction, having not received any replies to his earlier torrent of abuse, had given up and at last fallen silent. He sat miserably as the wagon lurched from side to side, throwing him back and forth. The second wagon followed less than a minute later. A glum and tearful Googie sat silently inside it. She had not uttered a word the whole trip.

As Ella had instructed, both wagons took the left fork in the road at the bridge, taking a loop that would bring them in a wide arc right back to the palace.

CHAPTER TWENTY-SIX

Princess Ella stood in front of the assembled VIPs.

"I want to say thank you from all Gabslandians for spending the day here with us," she began.

"I'm sorry to interrupt," said Simon, "but could we wait for Googie to arrive before we start? I don't want to cause a fuss, but we have a policy of maximum inclusion and I would hate for her to miss out on this final gathering."

"While we're at it, anyone seen Major Junction?" bellowed Spudbug. "He's probably still boo-hoo-hoo-ing over not being able to jump a single jump on his titchy horse, but he ought to be here."

"I have word that they are both on their way," said Ella. "And we have factored their late arrival into the timetable. So the unveiling..."

"Where are they?" shouted Spudbug. "What's going on?"

Ella looked to Frank, who nodded his encouragement. "Please bear with us," said Ella. "We have something special for you before the unveiling and, of course, we need to discuss matters of money. We still have great hopes for a positive outcome."

Spudbug folded her arms and narrowed her eyes. All the Spams sitting with her narrowed their eyes too. It was an unnerving sight and left Ella and Frank under no illusion as to the Spams' current thinking. King Fabian's behaviour had shown conclusively, they felt, that he was completely unfit to rule.

Simon and the Hipneys gave Ella a smile. That, in its own way, was just as condemning as the Spams' sullenness. Ella knew only too well that the Hipneys would remain polite and friendly right until the moment that they applied the *coup de grâce*. In fact, the friendlier they became, the greater the danger.

"You've been wonderful hosts," said Simon. "Please do continue."

"Thank you," said Ella. "So, before we reveal the topiary statue, we have Gabsland's greatest storyteller to spin his magic..."

"A story!" mocked Spudbug. "What are we – three years old?"

"How wonderful!" said Simon. "We Hipneys

adore the Arts."

"Please welcome," said Ella, trying to ignore the interruptions, "Frank!"

There was a polite but underwhelming ripple of applause. King Fabian shouted "Yeah!" and then, "Who's Frank?"

Frank walked on to the small platform they were using as a stage. As he and Ella crossed she gave him an encouraging smile. Frank's mouth was so dry that even though he attempted to smile back, his lips wouldn't unstick from each other.

He faced the dignitaries and noticed that Cook was there at the back. And Daisy. Even Small Dods had ventured out from underground for the first time in Frank's lifetime. He had two men with him who were wearing heavy disguise, but Frank knew they

must be Dimmock and Roger by the way they
stood. Especially by the way Roger stood —
hands on hips and head thrown back. The

palace gardeners, maids, stable hands, the women and men who worked in the laundry – everyone had come to witness this historic moment. They knew their futures were about to be decided, for good or ill, and no one wanted to miss it.

Frank closed his eyes and began. **"In a small house in a town not far from here there once lived a family of *giraffes...*"**

"GIRAFFES?" yelled Spudbug mockingly. **"All that's happening in the world and this kid is telling us a story about giraffes?"**

"Shhhh," said Simon. **"I like giraffes."**

Frank took a deep breath and started again. **"In a small house in a town not far from here there once lived a family of giraffes. They had built themselves a sweet little giraffe house to their own very specific giraffe specifications.**

The ceilings were lofty, the doors tall and narrow and, despite being as tall as a regular two-storey house inside, there was only a ground floor. No stairs. The kitchen cupboards, fridge and sink were high up near the roof at the ideal height for the giraffes to make themselves a drink or grab some food with their mouths.

"It was perfect for the giraffes and they lived happily there for many years in blissful solitude until one day a family of leopards turned up and started to build a house next door. The leopards built their house on stilts and filled it with log walkways and a cosy den. The giraffes were impressed and decided to visit the leopards to welcome them to the neighbourhood. They soon discovered that the leopards behaved very differently to the giraffes, who did nothing much but eat and stand around all day. The leopards were often much more active. 'Makes a nice change,' the giraffes said to each other. Not only that, but the leopards organized themselves into a strict order from the most important to the least important and every one of them knew their place in that order. They were often aggressive and menacing towards leopards lower in the order. The giraffes noticed that a leopard, when picked on by a superior, would turn on the next one down in the pecking order and take it out on him. Then, that one would take it out on the one below him and so on. All this fighting seemed odd to the giraffes, and unlike the behaviour of leopards they had met before, but they didn't feel it was their place to comment so they welcomed their new neighbours and tried to be as pleasant to them as they could.

"All was fine, and the giraffes and the leopards happily lived side by side until one day a family of crocodiles arrived and started to build themselves a house on the other side of the giraffes. Theirs was a wide, squat house, only a metre high. Once again the giraffes came to say hello to their new neighbours and the first thing they noticed about the crocodiles was their huge toothy grins. They had the biggest smiles the giraffes had ever seen. They were also extremely polite. 'What lovely new neighbours we have,' the giraffes said to each other. 'Aren't we lucky?'

"The crocodiles sometimes confided that they might quite enjoy eating the leopards, but the giraffes always persuaded the crocodiles to leave the leopards in peace. And the leopards sometimes confided that the crocodiles annoyed them with their big toothy smiles and they'd like to drive them away, but the giraffes always persuaded the leopards to leave the crocodiles in peace.

"And so more years passed without trouble until one year the giraffes had a baby boy and he was born with an unusually short neck. 'How interesting!' the giraffes said to each other. 'How strange!' the crocodiles said. 'How disgusting!' the leopards remarked.

"The giraffe, who they called Neckalas, grew and grew but his neck did not, and he was never able to reach the food in the cupboards at the top of the giraffe house. 'No problem!' the giraffes said. 'We will simply pass food and water to Neckalas whenever he needs it.' 'How odd!' said the crocodiles. 'How weak!' said the leopards.

"Eventually, Neckalas became the oldest and the most senior giraffe in the giraffe house and always the other giraffes were happy to pass him food and water when he needed it. The leopards still occasionally contemplated destroying the crocodile house and the crocodiles still occasionally contemplated eating the leopards, but the giraffes always talked them out of it."

"I hope *someone* is going to eat someone else in this story soon!" said Spudbug. "It'll be a big disappointment otherwise."

"Shh," said Simon.

"One day," continued Frank, "a leopard called Leonard encountered a crocodile called Crocabilly by the watering hole. Leonard was in a foul mood.

"'What's up?' asked Crocabilly. 'Enormous Derek has been horrible to me again,' complained Leonard. Enormous Derek was the most senior leopard. Leonard was second in line, but that didn't stop Enormous Derek regularly humiliating him.

"'I know just how you feel,' said Crocabilly. 'Hard Croc is *always* having a go at me. Look, I have an idea. We need our own place. We need to be our own bosses. Why don't we get rid of that weird Neckalas and his family and then you and I could move into their house. You'd be the only leopard and I'd be the only crocodile so we would have no one to tell us what to do – it'd be heaven!'

"'That's not a bad idea. I'll go and suggest it to Enormous Derek.'

"'Are you nuts?' said Crocabilly. 'Enormous Derek won't want you to become your own boss and have your own house. He enjoys torturing you too much. We must be cleverer than that. We must make him and Hard Croc think getting rid of Neckalas is *their* idea.'

"'How do we do that?' asked Leonard.

"'We make Neckalas seem more of a pain than he is,' Crocabilly replied.

"'A pain in the neck?' said Leonard.

"'This is no time for jokes!' Crocabilly

groaned. 'We make him seem such a nuisance that Enormous Derek and Hard Croc feel they have no choice but to get rid of him.'

"'How do we do that?'

"'Don't worry,' said Crocabilly, 'I've got a plan.'

"For the next few weeks, Crocabilly and Leonard made Neckalas' life a misery. They placed thorns on the ground that got stuck in his feet, causing him to stagger about howling in pain. They threw itching powder over him as he slept so that he snorted and cried out at night, keeping everyone awake. They contaminated his food so that he couldn't stop pooing all over the place. He became a huge nuisance not just to the other giraffes but to the crocodiles and the leopards too.

"Eventually, Enormous Derek and Hard

Croc had had enough and they drove Neckalas and his family away. Without the giraffes there to keep the peace, the leopards and the crocodiles soon started to fall out. Eventually they all either left or got eaten. To this day, those three empty houses stand as a monument to greed and treachery. A once peaceful, thriving community destroyed by ambition and intolerance."

There was silence. Frank looked out at the assembled dignitaries.

"Well that was depressing," said Spudbug.

"Yes, I feel miserable too," said Simon.

"What was the point of all that?" said Spudbug. "Couldn't you just let off some fireworks like normal people?"

"Well," said Frank, anxious because he knew that what he was about to say would change everything. "I told that story because that is what is happening here. In Gabsland, Spamon and Hipnia."

"What are you talking about?" said Spudbug.

"We're the giraffes, the Spams are the leopards and the Hipneys are the crocodiles. I'm saying that there are similarities between my story and what is actually happening here. There are people trying to stir up trouble. Big trouble. You and Simon are Enormous Derek and Hard Croc. King Fabian is Neckalas. And we have our own Leonard and Crocabilly."

"Who?" asked Simon.

"Major Junction and Googie," said Frank, barely audibly.

"Who?" shouted Spudbug.

"Major Junction and Googie," said Frank

more loudly. "Against your wishes, they have conspired to make King Fabian appear to be incompetent and – and weird."

The effect on the crowd was electric.

Spudbug ran to the stage, shoving over a couple of Spams that were in her way and seized Frank by the hair. "You are accusing my right-hand man of treason? I'm going to kill you!"

"We don't like violence," said Simon coldly. "But once you have had a turn strangling Frank we would like a go. How dare he accuse a Hipney of such criminal behaviour? Besides, the king ruined today all on his own."

"He **didn't!**" whimpered Frank. "Yes, he's eccentric – with all due respect, Your Majesty – but what is wrong with that? I know there is an issue with money, but you have to look at the bigger picture. What we do here in Gabsland is provide stability; we are a calming influence on your rivalry. Look at what's happened today – you've all been spending time together and you've got on pretty well. Haven't you? All things considered? Major Junction and Googie have been working together to bring that to an end. Spudbug and Simon didn't really want to place Gabsland into more trouble than it's already in, but those two did. I don't know why, but they did. So they did their best to make it happen – they drugged the king's cake, they put biting ants in his necklace. They want that money repaid at any cost and they are prepared to do anything to make it happen!"

"You liar," snarled Spudbug. "Why, I'll..."

"Stop!" shouted Ella. "We can prove it!"

Spudbug released his grip and threw Frank to the floor. "How?"

"You'll see," said Ella. "But we can only do so on one condition."

"Go on."

"We are going to bring Googie and Major Junction here without them knowing. They think they are many miles away from the palace on their way to our prison. We are going to bring them here and we must all stay utterly silent so as not to give the game away. If they suspect they are being overheard then this will not work and you will never know the truth."

"This is ridiculous," said Simon.

Spudbug cracked her knuckles ominously.

"Yes, you could refuse to believe us," Ella

went on. "Yes, you could storm out of here. Yes, you could call in the debts, seize our lands. But you will never know if you can trust Googie or Major Junction again. More importantly, without finding out the truth, justice will not be served. And I know you, Spudbug, and you, Simon, to be people of honour who believe in both justice and the rule of law."

"I've never heard such tripe," said Spudbug sourly.

"Is this some kind of trick?" asked Simon.

"It is not. I give you my word as a princess,"

said Ella.

"**And I give you my word as a kitchen boy,**" said Frank, immediately realizing that might not be the clincher he was hoping it would be.

Spudbug looked from one to the other and then to Simon, who shrugged.

"**Fine,**" said Spudbug. "**You have one chance to show us that this ridiculous story is true. But let me tell you this: if you cannot prove it, we will lock you and Frank up and we will throw away the key. We will demand every single penny that we are owed and if that means we have to seize this palace or even seize your whole country then we will do it. You owe us that money and we will have it back. If you are wrong about this, all Gabslandians, including you, in fact, *especially* you, will be miserable for ever more. Do you understand?**"

"And we will help the Spams to do whatever's necessary, just more politely," Simon added.

Frank and Ella nodded. Ella turned and waved a white handkerchief towards the woods far off on the other side of the pond.

"Please sit, everyone, and absolute silence until I give the all-clear," said Ella.

She and Frank took their seats in the front row, Spudbug sat next to them and Simon next to her. Frank looked to Ella, who gave him a reassuring nod and a smile. She was not feeling as confident as she looked.

Then, one of the wagons slowly lumbered out of the dark woods towards them. Three acrobats pushed it across the palace lawn towards the waiting group. As the wheels crossed the grass, the acrobats bounced the wagon up and down and rocked it from side to side so that the person inside would not be aware they were now crossing a smooth manicured lawn. At a couple of points one of the acrobats even let one of the wheels run over his foot to simulate a bumpy road. The acrobats wheeled the wagon close to the seated guests. At the open end of the wagon they could clearly see the forlorn figure of Major Junction, hands tied and bound to the bench, a heavy black cloth hood over his head. He had no idea that they had travelled in a large circle right back to where they had started. As far as he was concerned they were miles from the palace by now. One of the acrobats was chatting away.

"Finally," he said, **"water! I'm so thirsty I could drink a horse!"**

"That's not the expression, you goof," said

another. "It's 'I'm so thirsty I could drink a cow.'"

"Whatever," said the first. "I'm going to go over to the waterfall and drink. You coming?"

"There are the others!" shouted the second. "HELLO!"

This second wagon drew up alongside the first and there was Googie, tied, bound and hooded like Major Junction.

"Who's coming for a swim in the river?" asked one of the second group of acrobats.

"Try and stop me," said another. "I'm boiling."

"I'd better stay and keep an eye on the prisoners," said another.

"Nah, they'll be all right. They're tied up well. They're not going anywhere. Last one there's a smelly cheese!"

And all six acrobats took off across the lawn, laughing and shouting all the way so that Googie and Major Junction could hear them getting further and further away.

Then there was silence.

Ella and Frank had their mouths open and both were holding their breath. Spudbug's eyes were increasingly narrowed. Simon had his hands over his mouth. Queen Charlotte, arms crossed about her chest, had one eye open. King Fabian was looking at the stone statue of himself, wondering if Hindgut had made his ears too big.

Googie shifted slightly in her seat and everyone looked over to her. But then she slumped back down. Major Junction hadn't moved a muscle.

Seconds passed.

Nothing happened.

The seconds turned into minutes.

Nothing happened.

Spudbug turned to Ella and raised her eyebrows. Ella knew what she was implying – all this looked like was two upset, unjustly imprisoned high-ranking people.

More minutes passed.

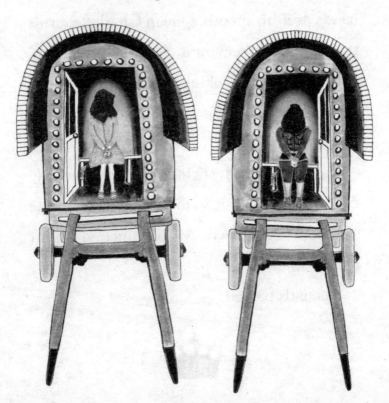

Nothing happened.

Ella felt tears welling up in the corners of her eyes. What had she done? This was the most stupid miscalculation of her life. Actually, no, she realized, not just the most stupid thing she had done in her life, but the most stupid thing anyone had ever done in any life in the history of the human race. She had gambled on this little trick saving her country, but she was about to put all Gabslandians in an even worse position than they were in before. Spudbug, she didn't doubt, would be as good as her word and, if anything, Simon looked angrier than Spudbug.

She had gambled – and she had lost. It was time to admit it. Ella bowed her head and stood up. She turned to face the group.

"Major!"

333

Ella froze. The voice had come from behind her. She wheeled round to face the wagons. Everyone held their breath.

Nothing.

Please, thought Ella. *Please, please, please speak.*

"What do you want?" said the major. Unmistakably! Out loud! They'd started speaking! Ella was so excited she nearly clapped her hands together in joy. Luckily she restrained herself. Frank was so tense and nervous he grabbed Ella's upper arm.

"What do I want?" said Googie. **"I want your head on a spike!"**

"Well you've got it!" hissed Major Junction. **"Congratulations."**

"I hope you rot," said Googie.

"Charming!"

"I should never have trusted you. All those bites I got collecting fire ants!"

"Oh, big deal. I was the one who had to get them into that orb and work out how to package them so they'd only come out at the right time! Do you have any idea how difficult that was?"

"I can't believe I ever listened to you!" said Googie. "I knew it wouldn't work! You don't have what it takes to pull this off."

"Don't have what it takes! I'm not the one who confessed everything to the bishop and blew the whole thing out of the water."

"What?!" Googie was screaming now. "What are you talking about? *YOU* confessed!!"

"No, you confessed!!"

"No, you did!"

"I didn't!"

335

"Well, I didn't either!"

They both fell silent as the truth hit them. They'd been tricked by Ella and Frank.

"Why that sneaky little..."

"Hang on," said Googie slowly. "If neither of us confessed then they have no proof. Once Spudbug and Simon hear about this they'll demand our release!"

"You're right! If anything, we'll be heroes! And they'll demand Gabsland pays back all its debts because they'll both be so furious! And what will that mean?"

"Money," whispered Googie.

"All that money," said the major. "All that beautiful money."

They both chuckled. Spudbug went to speak but Ella quickly raised a hand to stop her.

"Just in time for my turn as the country's

treasurer," said Googie. "Those idiots won't notice when half of it goes missing."

"My lot will eventually notice that I walked off with all the money," said Major Junction, "but far too late to do anything about it. We'll be long gone. It's going to be *amazing*! This will make it even easier to pull this off. We'll be heroes!"

"I just wish I could be there when they realize what we've done. The Spams are so stupid."

"Not as stupid as Spudbug," said Major Junction. "She thinks she's so clever but I run rings around her. I've stepped in cowpats that are smarter than her."

That was enough for Spudbug. She marched over to Major General and roughly pulled the hood from his head, nearly taking his ears off with it. Simon was over at Googie at the same time and removed her hood, in a slightly – but only ever so slightly – more gentle way.

The look on the two of their faces was something Frank would never forget for the rest of his life.

Pandemonium ensued.

It took eight men to pull Spudbug off her second in command. She was as ferocious as a wild animal. Major Junction was fortunate to escape with his life.

Simon and the other Hipneys immediately

held an emergency committee meeting and issued the most rapidly agreed statement in their history condemning Googie and calling for a national week of reflection.

Queen Charlotte had fainted, which she was later extremely pleased about once she woke up, because it meant she really had appeared lifeless at one of the most important moments in Gabslandian history.

King Fabian, shouting **"The suspense is killing me!"**, rushed over to the shrouded topiary statue and whipped the large sheet off, revealing three giraffes with their necks entwined – one with Fabian's face, one with Simon's and one with Spudbug's. The king took it in for a moment before declaring, **"At least I'm not wetting myself in this one!"**

Roger pulled off his disguise and boomed,

"It is I! Roger the under-butler!" to general indifference.

Frank and Ella quietly stood side by side as the yelling and shouting had erupted. Ella said, after a while, **"Do you think you could let go of my arm now please?"**

Frank did so. They didn't know whether to laugh or to cry. So they did both.

CHAPTER TWENTY-SEVEN

The events of that day changed the lives of everyone there and thousands who weren't.

The Spams, the Hipneys and the Gabslandians had no difficulty in immediately agreeing to an extension to the loans. Having seen how close they were to chaos and how easily they had been led there, all were keen for such a breakdown in relations to never occur again. They stayed at the palace for another month to firmly establish good relations.

King Fabian had all the dead animal heads removed from the dining room. He also conceded that he was not a natural leader and was nothing without Dimmock. He told the truth about his heroism and diplomacy – which was that he had none at all. He also revealed the two things on which he had spent all that money. The first was the palace topiary. He had employed hundreds of gardeners to come in secretly at night and keep the shapes and figures in the garden looking perfect.

"It would drive me potty," he said, "if any of the shapes had even one leaf out of line. I couldn't bear it. And plants grow every day so I wanted them to be trimmed every single day. I knew Dimmock wouldn't approve of the expense so I kept borrowing more and more money and I had the gardeners sneak in at night."

He had also spent a fortune on buying small porcelain figures of shepherdesses with sheep and goats.

"They are so beautiful – I couldn't stop," said the king.

He had led Dimmock to a room in the attic and there were over twelve thousand of them. The king agreed to sell them all and the money raised helped to lower the debt considerably. He agreed that he probably wasn't the best leader for the country and arranged for an election to pick a prime minister. Dimmock was elected by a huge majority and ruled with wisdom and compassion for a long while, paying off the debt in full within a few years.

Queen Charlotte came to realize that being dead could wait until she actually was. She also realized that her daughter was well worth spending time with. But she still favoured wearing black dresses and pale make-up.

Roger was offered the role of butler once Dimmock became a politician and he accepted. His first day on the job was serving at the banquet held to mark the end of the month's visit of the Spams and the Hipneys. The moment he and Spudbug locked eyes sparks flew. They fell instantly and hopelessly in love. Roger travelled back to Spamon, married Spudbug and set up the first ever Spam theatre, in which he always took the leading role.

Cook was asked to name her prize for her part in the apprehension of Googie and asked for a new set of knives. She wept with joy when she was given them, sobbing, **"As my old uncle used to say, 'A new set of knives a day keeps the**

doctor away.'" They remain sharp to this day.

Small Dods had not enjoyed his first trip outside in years and returned underground, never to see daylight again. His cells remained empty for the next eight years until one of the gardeners was caught having a wee into the royal fountain and was sent to spend a night in the dungeon. The gardener's defence – that he was just copying the king – was not accepted by the judge. Small Dods spent the night lecturing the gardener on his dangling participles.

Frank was offered any job he cared to ask for in the palace but decided to remain the kitchen boy. He enjoyed the work and it gave him time to think up his stories. He did, however, ask for every Wednesday afternoon off so that he could begin to write his stories down in a book.

And Ella was never lonely again. She now

had a friend in Frank, and the two of them would play and laugh together whenever they could. Ella worked hard studying law and wrote Gabsland's first constitution which ensured that no royal would ever again hold power.

Would things have turned out this way if King Fabian had not farted and then denied it? Who knows? All we can say with any certainty is that from little actions mighty events can result.

Perhaps, if (and when) *you* next fart, just say **"excuse me"** and get on with your day. You have no idea the trouble you might avoid...

ACKNOWLEDGEMENTS

Let me first make this clear: the fart that kicks off the mayhem in this book was not inspired by any single real-world fart. I can lay neither the praise nor the blame (depending on your view of farting) for the inspiration for this book's inciting event at anyone's back door. I'm not going to thank the farters of the world because that's everyone on the planet, but I am going to thank the people who disapprove of farting because that helps to make farting even funnier for the rest of us.

On second thoughts, perhaps I should have ended with the farting stuff.

Anyway. My sister Anita has, again, done an incredible job with the illustrations. She brings the book to life. And she's an absolute joy to work with. Thanks, sis. Lauren Fortune, my editor, has guided me, encouraged me and told me to get on with it with the utmost subtlety, intelligence and sensitivity. This book owes her a huge debt. Thanks too to Sarah Dutton, Aimee Stewart and everyone at Scholastic who worked so hard to get this book into shape. Thanks to Penelope Daukes, who is so brilliant at getting the word out there and does it with such grace and good-humour. Thanks to Peter Nixon for his continued support, encouragement and wise counsel and to Paul Stevens for his expert guidance.

And finally thanks to my son, Frank, who donated both his name and his powerful and fertile imagination to the lead character. Your mind contains riches in abundance, Frank. And thanks for being such a good sport about lending your name to a book about a fart.

Sorry.

Not sorry.

Photo © Idil Sukan

STEPHEN MANGAN is a Tony-nominated actor known for his roles in *Green Wing, I'm Alan Partridge* and *Episodes*. Stephen also voiced the title role in *Postman Pat: The Movie*. He was a member of the judging panel for the 2020 Costa Book of the Year prize.

@StephenMangan

ANITA MANGAN is a successful illustrator and designer who has worked on award-winning books for the Leon brand, Gizzi Erskine, Fearne Cotton, Ella's Kitchen, Comptoir Libanais and the bestselling *'Be a Unicorn, Sloth, Flamingo...'* series.

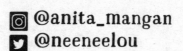

@anita_mangan
@neeneelou

DON'T MISS:

Turn over for a sneak peek. . .

Don't look down, Jack told himself, *just don't look down.*

The man, Jack had already forgotten his name, unbolted the gate and swung it open. He fixed it in place. There was now nothing between Jack and the drop. The woman, who Jack thought was called Tilly, gave him an encouraging smile.

Why had he agreed to this? Even now, he wasn't sure.

He placed his hands on the railing and shuffled his feet forward until his toes poked over the edge. He glanced down and immediately wished he hadn't.

Far, far below him was the fair: the carousel, the little roller coaster, the Waltzer.

The cage swayed in the breeze. It was quiet up here. Odd sounds drifted up, people screaming on the Pirate Ship, a mishmash of music, a siren in the distance. Above them, the cables attaching the cage to the crane creaked and groaned.

The long elastic rope hung beneath.

Jack looked for his dad. He wasn't hard to spot. The only person standing still in a stream of fairgoers, poring over his phone, flicking through the photos of Jack he'd taken minutes earlier, oblivious to the inconvenience he was causing.

He'd have a heart attack if he knew I was up here, thought Jack.

Jack glanced behind him. The man and Tilly gave him a nod. He took a deep breath. As he had been instructed, he lifted his arms straight in front of him and leaned forward.

His throat was dry. He felt sweat prickle all over his body.

I could still stop this, he thought. He hadn't yet got to the point of no return. He could turn around. There was still time to place his hands back on the railing and say to Tilly, "I've changed my mind. I've decided I don't want to throw myself head-first out of a stupidly high cage, suspended from a stupidly big crane, and fall through the air towards the stupidly hard ground. Sorry, I don't know what I was thinking."

He could still have done that. But he didn't.

He leaned forward. His mind was racing but his body moved in slow motion. When you lean forward, he noticed, the first bit happens quite slowly: you're just leaning forward. But it'll get to the point where gravity takes over and the slow lean forward will become a breakneck plunge.

I think I'm past the point where I can stop this, he thought.

Yes, I am definitely past that point now. I'm going to fall.

Without thinking, Jack bent his knees and jumped, throwing his body forward into space, flinging his arms out wide like wings.

From a distance, it looked graceful, majestic, but no one was watching. Now upside down and falling freely, Jack straightened his arms above his head and held his body in a perfect line, an Olympic diver about to enter the water.

He fell, picking up speed at an incredible rate, the wind roaring in his ears, cold and loud. Faster and faster.

This is where the rope tightens, he thought, *this is where the rope stops me falling and I bounce back up again. They just leave it to the last minute to make it extra exciting.*

Right about now. . .

The ground rushed towards him, and it looked like there might be no way he could stop in time. Was this the thrill of it? Was this why people did it? Feeling you were going to hit the ground and then at the last moment – phew! – saved. The rope would tighten, he'd slow to a brief stop and then be thrown into reverse, back up into the sky, and it would all be over.

Any moment now.

Now?

Oh no. . .

Arrow-straight, arms and fingers extended, body vertical, mouth open, Jack hit solid ground at high speed.

And went right through it, with a small,

muffled *plop*.

Like dropping a bowling ball into a vat of jelly.

The ground folded around him and swallowed him up.

There was no trace of any impact, no sign that the earth had been disturbed.

The only clue as to what had happened was the tight, quivering elastic rope coming out of the ground, connected to the cage far above.

That was not how Jack had thought his evening was going to pan out.

Earlier on, Jack and his dad had gone to the funfair, the way they always did on Jack's birthday. Jack hadn't really wanted to, not this year, but his dad had insisted. And during the evening his dad had taken a lot of photos of Jack. Way more than normal. He wasn't good at taking pictures. His technique was to point his phone and click away, hoping that one of them would turn out to be good. The photos Jack's dad had taken in front of the Sky Scream were the final straw.

"You finished, Dad?"

"**Just one more. And smile, Jack!** Not like that, that looks fake. Smile normally. No, that looks creepy."

Jack had wanted to explain that his smile didn't look real because it wasn't real, but he had said nothing. He often said nothing. It was easier that way.

This particular photo session had been especially embarrassing not just because they were at the funfair, surrounded by crowds of people, but because behind his dad a group of six boys from Jack's school had been queueing at Sizzlers burger van. Jack hoped they wouldn't see him. He used to hang around with these boys and he used to really make them laugh. But lately they had started to avoid him, not inviting him to the park after school or to play at their houses.

Jack couldn't blame them. He wasn't much fun these days.

Fortunately, they were otherwise engaged trying to snatch the hat off the head of the smallest boy, Niblet. Niblet was not enjoying the game at all. They always picked on Niblet.

The stench of frying onions and vinegar coming from Sizzlers was making Jack feel queasy. He risked a glance over to the boys.

Niblet had finally lost his cool and punched Beano in the arm. Beano put Niblet in a headlock. Beano was called Beano because he could inhale a baked bean via his nostril

and often did.

Jack's dad had wanted them to go on the Sky Scream, the scariest ride in the whole fair.

"No way," Jack had said, but his dad wasn't having that and had tried to get Jack to change his mind.

"Oh, come on, Jack, surely you want to try it?"

"I'm good thanks, Dad."

"Oh, Jack-Jack. You don't want me telling everyone you were too scared, do you?"

"I suppose not."

"You'll love it once you're actually on it!"

"Nah, I'm OK."

"Jack, you're annoying me now, just go on the ride!"

"Let's do a different one..."

"Come on, J, please."

"Seriously, Dad, I don't want to."

His dad sulked. **"If you don't go on that ride we're going home."**

"That's fine by me."

"Well, that's ridiculous, all the money I've spent on you tonight. You're acting like a child."

Jack had wanted to say, "I *am* a child," but he didn't. Instead, he said something much worse.

"Mum wouldn't make me go on it."

For a moment there was silence.

Jack had brought up his mum. That was the nuclear option. It got him out of the argument, but it was too big a weapon for this fight. A bomb that had taken them both out. They had both lost.

"Let's just take a photo in front of it then, shall we?" Dad said weakly, forcing a smile. Jack had posed for the photo but felt wretched.

Jack didn't want to be at the fair, and Jack

knew his dad didn't want to be there either. They were both trying to please each other but neither of them was happy.

When Mum was alive, it had been a family tradition to visit this fair each year on Jack's birthday. Coming this year was Jack's dad's way of saying things would be all right, things would carry on, that some things hadn't changed. But everything had changed.

The lads from his school had been served their food. Niblet sneaked up behind Beano as he was squirting ketchup on his burger and kicked it out of his hands. The meat, ketchup and onions arced through the air then splattered on to the flattened grass. Niblet sprinted off into the crowd, whooping with delight.

Jack's dad took yet another picture.

Jack had to get out of there.

"Dad, I need the loo," he lied.

Jack rushed off, but almost immediately the slow flow of people he had been impatiently trying to squeeze past had ground to a halt and he was stuck.

He looked back to see if he should give up on this idea and return to his dad, but there were as many people behind him as in front. Jack looked at the ground and sighed. He felt hopeless, again. He should have just gone on the ride so that this whole trip, this misjudged attempt of his father's to have fun, would have been over sooner and then they could have gone home and Jack could hide in his room again. Every decision he made at the moment seemed to be the wrong one.

Jack pushed his way through the mass of

people, hemmed in by dozens of anoraks and overcoats.

Just then, the crowd parted and Jack could see clearly. And there, in a gap between the fairground stalls, was a woman. She was watching him.

It was . . . his mum.

Jack froze; time slowed.

For one heartbeat the world stopped.

Jack stood and looked, unable to process what he was seeing.

The crowd surged forward, blocking Jack's view once more, and the world flooded back in – sound, breath and sensation.

No, was his first thought. *No. That's not her. It can't be her. She's dead.*

When the crowd parted again, she was gone. No woman, no mum, no one there. Had he imagined it? He had to find out. Jack headed towards the spot where he had seen her, a narrow passage between the fairground stalls that led towards a patch of woodland, and walked down it. Picking his way carefully across the thick electrical cables underfoot, he edged into the darkness.

Behind him the hustle and bustle of the fair faded away. He almost lost his balance in the gloom and, as he went to steady himself, was surprised by the loud *clang* his hand made as it slammed into the metal wall.

Emerging into a patch of open ground, his eyes took a moment to adjust to the darkness. The temperature felt noticeably cooler back here and the breeze smelled of wet grass and petrol.

There she was, walking away from him.

He went to call out, but no words came. He stumbled towards her, and just then she turned.

It wasn't her.

Of course, he thought, of course it wasn't. How could it have been? He felt foolish and embarrassed.

There was a bit of a resemblance, the same colour hair, about the same height but … it wasn't her.

"Do you want to do a bungee jump?" the woman asked.

Jack half-smiled and shook his head. "No way."

Behind the woman, in a metal cage that came up to his waist, stood a man holding a sign that read:

The cage was attached to an enormous crane.

"We're really not supposed to be here," said

the woman. "Can you keep a secret?"

The man and the woman smiled at Jack.

I should leave, Jack thought.

"I don't like heights," he said. "I'm going now."

But he didn't.

"I'm not doing a bungee jump," he said, walking over to the cage as though pushed by invisible hands. "I watched my dad do one once. It took him ages to jump. He said you can't believe how high up you are, and your body and mind are screaming, **'DANGER!!'** and every fibre of your being is telling you not to do it. So, yeah, it's not really for me, free or not."

He stepped into the cage through the little metal gate held open for him by the man.

"I'm Tilly, that's Bobby," the woman said. "Do you want to do a bungee jump? You don't have to."

"No. I don't. Absolutely not!" Jack laughed and Tilly laughed too.

They stood, smiling at each other.

Then Jack found himself saying this:

"Well, I suppose I could do one. Why not?"